DEARLY DEPARTED

Mary put the lid on her cookies. "I can't believe Summer and Auntie are gone or that Auntie made such a mistake."

"You know, my dear, if it wasn't an accident," the Professor said, "it means suicide or someone murdered them."

We all sat up straighter at the word *murdered*.

"Well... well..." Mary seemed at a loss for words. "I just meant she knew her plants. It doesn't seem possible..."

"Not suicide for either of them," Gertie said. "Auntie was a devout Greek Orthodox, and Summer was committed to saving Mark."

"The process of elimination means someone killed them," Martha stated.

With her strident voice, the word *killed* leapt out. I doubted any of us wanted to go down that path, but there it was. The fork in the road. Accept that it was an accident, mourn them, and move on, or take a step toward a dark place where people took the lives of others...

Books by Janet Finsilver

MURDER AT REDWOOD COVE

MURDER AT THE MANSION

MURDER AT THE FORTUNE TELLER'S TABLE

Published by Kensington Publishing Corporation

Murder at the Fortune Teller's Table

Janet Finsilver

LYRICAL UNDERGROUND
Kensington Publishing Corp.
www.kensingtonbooks.com

LYRICAL UNDERGROUND BOOKS are published by

Kensington Publishing Corp.
119 West 40th Street
New York, NY 10018

All Kensington titles, imprints, and distributed lines are available at special quantity discounts for bulk purchases for sales promotion, premiums, fund-raising, educational, or institutional use.

Special book excerpts or customized printings can also be created to fit specific needs. For details, write or phone the office of the Kensington Sales Manager: Kensington Publishing Corp., 119 West 40th Street, New York, NY 10018. Attn. Sales Department. Phone: 1-800-221-2647.

Lyrical Underground and Lyrical Underground logo Reg. US Pat. & TM Off.

First Electronic Edition: March 2017
eISBN-13: 978-1-61650-933-0
eISBN-10: 1-61650-933-3

First Print Edition: March 2017
ISBN-13: 978-1-61650-934-7
ISBN-10: 1-61650-934-1

Printed in the United States of America

To my husband, E.J., for his understanding and support.

ACKNOWLEDGMENTS

I want to thank my husband for being there for me as I wrote *Murder at the Fortune Teller's Table*. We were remodeling our home and went through some hectic times. I appreciate all the feedback from my fabulous writing group made up of Colleen Casey, Staci McLaughlin, Ann Parker, Carole Price, and Penny Warner. I want to give a special thanks to my Greek friend, Georgia Drake, who shared her knowledge of Greek customs with me. I am grateful to Mario Abreu, staff naturalist at the Mendocino Coast Botanical Gardens, for sharing his knowledge of poisonous plants with me and to Greg Firman for helping me with the military information in this book. I'm fortunate to work with a great agent, Dawn Dowdle, and a wonderful editor, John Scognamiglio. Thank you all!

Chapter 1

I stepped out of my Jeep and stopped to marvel at the colorful Redwood Cove scene before me. Brightly hued banners rippled in the ocean breeze, and tables covered with multicolored cloths dotted the green lawn. Baked goods, jars of honey and jam, and an assortment of knitted scarves and hats filled the one nearest me. Groups of kids wearing school sweatshirts darted between groups of milling adults. In the distance, the Pacific Ocean glistened in the early-afternoon sun.

"Miss Kelly! Miss Kelly!" Tommy Rogers's frantic waving to get my attention made him look like he was doing jumping jacks. The electric company would make money if they could figure out a way to tap into the blond ten-year-old's boundless energy.

I headed toward him and his mother, Helen. A bit of gray graced her brown hair. "Glad you could make it," she said.

"The guests have all checked in. Redwood Cove Bed-and-Breakfast has a full house tonight," I said.

"The themed rooms you thought up have really attracted people."

"I'm glad Michael liked my idea and decided to give it a chance."

When I had proposed the plan to my boss, Michael Corrigan, owner of Resorts International, he'd raised an eyebrow, tilted his head, and said, "Sure. Let's do it and see what happens." I remembered my excitement. It was my first suggestion as the new manager for the property . . . and the beginning of my new career.

"My cell phone works in town, so I left a note on the door if anyone has questions," I said.

"I'll leave in time to get the food and drink ready." Helen lived on site and worked at the inn as a general assistant as well as preparing breakfast and the evening wine and cheese for the guests.

A tall, thin woman with wavy gray hair falling to her waist and a perky yellow daisy tucked behind her ear approached us. Soft hues swirled together on her long, flowing skirt, and she wore an embroidered vest over a peasant blouse. She smiled at me and turned to Helen. "Have you seen Mary Rutledge? She's going to give me a break this afternoon at Auntie's table."

Helen pointed to a row of displays next to a stand of redwoods. "She and Gertie Plumber are at the last table."

"Thanks."

"Summer, I'd like you to meet Kelly Jackson. She recently moved here to run Redwood Cove Bed-and-Breakfast."

The woman's gaze was as warm as the season she was named after. Her soft hand reached out and clasped mine with a light touch. "Pleased to meet you. My name is Amy Winter, but everyone calls me Summer."

Her nickname and the serene look she gave me were a perfect fit, reminding me of long, lazy days during the summer.

"Welcome to Redwood Cove," she said. "It's nice to meet you."

"Same here."

Summer floated off.

"Miss Kelly, look at my sweatshirt. My class made the design," Tommy said.

A dark gray whale swam on a light blue background, a white spout of spray trailing it.

"Everyone loved watching the whales migrate and learning about them. We used ideas from our projects for our booth and class banner." Tommy grabbed his mom's hand, tugging. "Come see what my class did."

"Okay. Let's go," Helen said, and I followed along.

Tommy stopped in front of a table decorated in a marine theme, swarming with blue-shirted children as they showed their parents their class display. I admired the artwork, declined a whale-shaped cookie thrust in my direction in the hand of an excited fifth-grader, and then said my good-byes. I drifted down the row of tables as Tommy began to explain a project in extensive, accurate detail to his mother, as he was prone to do with his touch of Asperger's syndrome.

A couple of displays down, I stopped to look at a brown satin banner featuring images of Native Americans. Someone had even added beads to their outfits. My gaze scanned the group, and I saw the back of a girl with straight, blue-black hair standing next to a man with high cheekbones and light brown skin. I recognized Allie Stevens and her father, Daniel. Until recently, he'd been a handyman at the inn. Now he managed a sister property, the Ridley House, and we often worked together on orders and events.

Daniel spied me and waved. "Welcome to our annual fund-raiser and get-to-know-your-school event."

"You have quite the turnout."

"The community is very supportive. We're lucky to live here."

Allie pointed to the flag. "I helped design it, and the class all wanted me to put in one of my ancestors to represent my tribe."

"It's stunning, Allie."

She beamed, a far cry from the angry teenager I'd first heard about when I arrived at Redwood Cove.

I surveyed the event, which was popping with color and action. "I'm going to wander around a bit. I'll catch you later."

"Sure thing." Daniel turned and helped tack up a poster. Another person was standing on a chair, struggling to put the placard in place, an easy task for Daniel with his height.

I strolled between the displays, soaking in the sun, occasionally stopping to inhale the fresh salty air. I stepped over to a row of tall redwoods lining the edge of the function and watched the seagulls soaring overhead. They dipped, dove, and spun on thermal drafts . . . a visual representation of my spirits. This was my new community, and I was thrilled at the smiling faces and outpouring of support I saw from the people of all ages before me.

Rejoining the crowd, I spied a couple of pairs of knit baby booties with rainbow designs. I ran my hand over their soft fabric. They'd be perfect for my sister's twins. Next to them, thick woolen scarves made me think of my brothers, and nearby hats brought images of Grandpa and Dad. A Wyoming cattle ranch in winter defined the word *cold*, and my family would appreciate these cozy items. A few booths down, I found handmade coasters made from wine corks. We opened the ranch to paying guests in the summer, and Mom could use these in their cabins.

I went looking for Mary and Gertie and found them, sun glinting off their silver hair, manning a table full of baked goods. Boxes of coconut-covered cookies and chocolate bars filled the area in front of Mary. Gertie had homemade loaves of a stout-looking bread. No surprise there. Mary loved her sweets, and Gertie's Pennsylvania Dutch background lent itself to hardy food.

"What do you think of our little gathering?" Mary asked, her round face lit with a smile.

"It's great. I've already started my Christmas shopping!" I held up the bag.

"Good-quality items, and the money helps the school," Gertie said. "I helped one class sew a quilt using scraps of leftover material. Maybe some of them will keep it up after this is over."

Two tan furry triangles appeared at the edge of the table next to Mary. They began to rise, revealing two large ears. The top of a brown head emerged, followed by two small dark eyes and a black nose. Then there was the jeweled collar. Rows of large pink crystals glittered in the sunlight.

"Princess, you need to stay in your carrier," Mary said.

Collar, head, and ears slowly sank out of sight.

I leaned over the table to get a better look at the dog—a little Chihuahua.

Mary reached over and petted the dog. "Good girl."

"Princess?" I hadn't seen her before.

Mary nodded. "My sister lived with me until recently, and Princess was her hearing-assistance dog. Princess is beginning to have some hearing problems herself, so she's now retired. We both raised her, and when my sister moved to Sacramento, Princess stayed with me."

"She's cute."

"Thanks." Mary glanced at her watch and turned to Gertie. "I need to go relieve Summer in about ten minutes. I said I'd help Auntie out so Summer could look around."

"Who's Auntie?" I asked.

"She's a Greek woman who has lived here for ages. Auntie tells fortunes, reading coffee grounds. It's a fascinating process. She also sells herbal remedies. Auntie used to be a midwife, but she no longer does that."

"Where's her table? I'd like to see how she does it." I wondered what the fortune teller would reveal about this next chapter in my life.

Mary gave me directions, and I headed out to discover my future. Auntie's table was off by itself, some distance away from the crowd. Summer and a pale man sat across from a woman in black, voluminous clothes, a cloth scarf on her head. She was staring into a small cup, and I could see her lips move.

Suddenly, Summer stood, and even at a distance, I heard her loud "No!" She turned to the man, who was now standing next to her, and grabbed his arm. She pulled him away from the table, and they headed in my direction.

The man put his arm around her shoulders as they walked by me. "Mom, it doesn't mean anything. It's coffee grounds and Auntie's active imagination."

Tears had pooled in Summer's eyes.

"You don't know." She shook her head from side to side and looked stunned. "The things I've seen come about."

"Mom, I have no dark secrets from the past that will be revealed," he said, his voice beginning to trail off as they moved away. "And no one is going to die."

Chapter 2

Dark secrets?
People dying?

I turned in the direction of the fortune teller. What had seemed like a fun lark had taken an ugly twist. Did I want to hear what she had to say about me? I was enjoying the beautiful day and was on top of the world with my job. What if she predicted problems? Failure? I'd struggled to find a place where I fit in, and this felt like it. I didn't want anything to mar the experience. I took a step back.

Mary came bubbling up beside me. "Oh, good. You're going to have your fortune told. It's fun!"

She swept me along with her, and the next thing I knew I found myself sitting at a table covered by a white crocheted tablecloth. Layers of black material covered the diminutive form across from me and rustled as she leaned forward. Folds of black formed a head-dress atop a deeply lined face. Each wrinkle spoke of a story to be told.

"You would like to know your future, yes?" Her voice was reedy.

I nodded, but my heart was in my throat.

"I am Despina Manyotis. Here I am called Auntie." A smile creased her face. "In my country, we read the patterns in the grounds of Turkish coffee to predict the future. It's a very ancient practice. Some people call it tasseography." She shrugged her shoulders. "To me it's fortune telling."

Mary had been bustling around a one-burner stove a short way behind the fortune teller. "The coffee's about ready."

"My hands, you see . . ." Auntie put her crooked hands on the delicate lace cloth. "I cannot handle the *briki*, the special pot for preparing the coffee, by myself anymore. Summer and Mary help me so I can continue to tell the future."

"It's done." Mary turned the burner off.

Auntie's gnarled hands pulled a white demitasse cup in front of her, and Mary filled it with hot, steaming coffee. "First you drink the coffee," Auntie said.

She pushed the cup over to me as Mary placed the long-handled, triangular-shaped copper pot on the table.

I took a sip of the dark, aromatic liquid. Auntie then nudged a plate of braided cookies in my direction. "These are *koulourakia*, made like in the old country."

Picking up a delicate braided treat, I nibbled on it. The buttery cookie melted in my mouth.

"You must drink from the same side of the cup for the entire process and leave a little in the bottom. With your last sip, make a wish."

I drank some more, then put the cup down with thoughts for a positive future. "Okay. There's just a little left."

"Now put the saucer on it upside-down, swirl it three times, and flip it over."

I did as instructed and managed to keep everything together when I upended it.

"Now it must rest for a short while." Her voice was a broken whisper, and I leaned forward to catch her words. "The grounds need to flow into their shapes."

She folded her hands and stared at the cup. After what seemed an eternity, Auntie carefully separated the cup and saucer. "The patterns—they tell of your past, present, and future. I see you are right-handed, so we start at the cup's handle and move from right to left."

She peered intently into the cup, moving it around, examining the sides and bottom. Then she inspected the saucer. Auntie nodded slowly.

I flinched each time she frowned, fidgeted when she stared fiercely into the cup and muttered, and cringed when she shouted "ha" a few times. Finally, she sat back. Her dark brown eyes looked at me from their creased folds. Her face transformed as a smile spread across it.

"You are like an eagle that has journeyed to find its aerie, the place it will call home. You landed, tucked in your wings, and have found your destination."

Whew! I almost fell off the chair with relief. Not that I believed in any of this stuff, but then again . . .

Mary had stayed in the background but now stepped forward. "What do you think? Did you enjoy it?"

I did now that it was over and the future looked bright. "Absolutely. Thank you, Auntie."

The woman gave a slight nod, then the glow left her face. She looked off in the direction Summer and her son had gone and crossed herself. "I'm through for the day." She rose, slowly unbending each part of her body to stand. "Summer will take care of this for me." A sweeping wave took in the table and the equipment.

She picked up her cane, a polished piece of wood with a knob on the end. "So good to meet you." Slowly she made her way to a trail winding through the grass and shuffled off.

I took a deep breath, glad the strange scene was over and my future looked sunny. My shoulders dropped a couple of inches. I hadn't realized how tense I was.

Mary put the coffeepot back on the stove. "I'll tidy up a bit to help Summer."

"Are the other Silver Sentinels here?" I'd spent quite a bit of time with the crime-solving group of senior citizens of which Mary and Gertie were members. We'd even named the conference room at the inn after them, in honor of the last case they'd helped solve.

"The Professor is helping the logistics team."

A perfect match for his organizational talents.

She then laughed. "Ivan and Rudy have a table where they're teaching people how to tie elaborate rope knots like they use on their boat, *Nadia*. They have samples and instruction sheets people can purchase."

"I thought I heard the boom of Ivan's voice." I mentally saluted the Russian Doblinksy brothers for their clever contribution to the day.

Mary pointed toward the front of the event. Even at a distance, I could see Ivan's bulk over the crowd.

"Thanks. I'll stop by and see you before I go."

Ivan was bending over the display table. A black cap with an ornate brocade band controlled his shaggy mane of gray hair.

"Ivan, I like your hat," I said.

He straightened up. "Welcome, Miss Kelly. Is my dress Russian fisherman's hat. Wear for special days."

His brother, Rudy, came over and stood next to him. He was a slight man with a neatly trimmed beard. "Would you like to make one?" He gestured at the examples they'd created.

Rows of knots lined the table with name cards. I might be able to figure out the clove hitch, but the rest of them looked beyond me, especially the angler's loop. On the ranch, all I needed was a quick-release knot for tying the horses and a honda knot to make a lasso.

"I'll pass, but I think you have a really smart idea for the event."

Copies of instructions were in a neat pile, weighed down by an abalone shell.

A young boy appeared to have all the fingers of his left hand wrapped in white cord. "Grandpa, what's next?"

The man hovering over him said, "Slip this piece of rope forward."

The two continued working together until the child yelled, "I did it! I did it! Thank you, Grandpa. Let's do another one."

The elderly man's face brightened as he grabbed another piece of twine.

It was a pleasure watching the two interact and to have the boy interested in working with his hands. I saw way too many kids staring at electronic devices instead of engaging in the world around them.

In addition to the examples, the brothers had completed knots, directions, and strands of rope for sale. I bought an angler's loop, instructions, and several lengths of white cord to put in the Maritime Suite at the inn. The guests might have fun trying to create the knot.

I said good-bye to the brothers and went to touch base with Mary and Gertie. As I approached their table, Summer showed up. The now-wilted daisy dangled from her ear.

"Mary," she said, "I need the help of the Silver Sentinels. I don't know how much you charge, but I'll find a way to pay you." She'd put on a shawl and clutched it tightly around her, distorting the knit pattern.

"Oh, honey, we don't charge. It's a service we provide to the townspeople."

Summer pulled harder on the garment; the yarn tightened and looked like the strings of an instrument. I thought the material might snap. "How soon can we meet?"

"What's it about?" Mary asked.

Summer shook her head—short, jerky movements. "Not here. Somewhere private."

"Okay." Mary came around the table and enveloped Summer in her soft, plump arms. "Whatever it is you need help with, we're here for you."

"Can we meet today? After the event?"

"Well, I don't know . . ." Mary stammered. "I don't know if everyone can make it."

Gertie piped up. "No reason to put it off if we can do it this afternoon."

I stepped forward. "I can check with the others, and I already know the conference room is available."

The desperate look on Summer's face dissipated a bit. "Would you do that? Please?"

"Sure. Happy to."

I left her pacing next to Mary.

Ivan and Rudy said they could make it. Next I had to find the Professor. That was a more challenging task. I headed for a man with a clipboard wearing a polo shirt with the name of the school district on it.

"I'm looking for Herbert Winthrop. Do you know where he is?"

"The Professor is helping collect the proceeds. The event is scheduled to be over in ten minutes. He was taking the first row of tables along the redwood trees."

I thanked him and went looking for the Professor. Retired from the University of California, Berkeley, he'd made it clear early on that he preferred the moniker of Professor over Herbert Winthrop. I walked over to a man in a brown tweed jacket with a matching wool hat and a box in his hand, talking to a vendor.

"Hi, Professor. Good to see you."

"Same to you, dear. I hope you are enjoying our little function."

"I am indeed."

He nodded his satisfaction.

"Professor, Amy Winter needs the help of the Sentinels. She's very anxious about something and wants to meet today, if possible. Will that work for you?"

"Yes. My obligation here won't keep me much longer."

"We'll meet in the conference room at the inn."

"I shall see you shortly then." He gave a good-bye wave with a tug at his cap.

When I returned, smashed grass showed the pattern of Summer's pacing. Her face had turned an ashen color. The sunny days of summer had disappeared as a storm of catastrophic proportions appeared to have engulfed her life. When she saw me, she stopped in her tracks. I thought she might crumble if the news wasn't what she hoped to hear.

"Everyone can meet. Let's make it an hour from now."

"Thank you. Thank you so much." Tears began to trickle down her cheeks.

I explained where we'd meet and hoped she heard me, considering the far-off look in her eyes.

"I must do it." Summer didn't say this to me, but to herself. "I must. I have no choice."

What must she do?

Chapter 3

"I must do it." Summer said the words over and over like some kind of mantra as she walked away.

I got in my Jeep and pulled out in a line of other cars. Making a left at the first intersection, I turned and headed down the hill. My breath caught as the white spire of Redwood Cove Bed-and-Breakfast came into sight, framed by the blue ocean beyond it. I'd never tire of this view.

The driveway went by the entrance to the inn. The flowers draping the front porch were their usual magnificent riot of blues, yellows, and reds hanging from lush green vines. The recently painted ornate white gingerbread trim popped out in vivid contrast to the colorful vegetation. I stopped, put down the window, and inhaled the perfumed air. Continuing on, I parked in the area near the back porch and entered the multiuse room.

Built in the 1880s by the Baxter family, this part of the house had been the servants' work area. When it was remodeled, the space became the heart of the building. A kitchen and dining area occupied the right side, while a sitting area with overstuffed chairs, a couch, and beanbag chairs was in front of me. The wood-burning stove filled the room with heat as well as provided the sight of cheerful flames dancing in the door's glass window. A large television set was in one corner. On my left, a large oak worktable enabled me to meet with staff and for us to have plenty of room for notes and papers. It handled larger groups for dining when necessary.

And I loved this part of the house.

The room had a welcoming warmth all its own. It embraced you like a mother beckoning you to come in and be part of the family, saying, "Join us and sit by the fire. Have a bite to eat." The sweet scent of baking lingered in it all day.

Fred, a tricolored basset hound, stretched out in his bed and yawned when I entered, his eyes never leaving the back door. I warranted a two-tail-thump greeting. Fred was so deeply engrossed in waiting for Tommy, I was impressed he even noticed me.

Helen looked up from the counter as she prepared the guests' appetizers. "Hi! Did you enjoy the school benefit?"

"Wonderful! The small-town environment and sense of community are what I grew up with. It's what feels like home to me."

"It's beginning to be a fit for me as well. As you know, it was tough in the beginning," she said. "We were both outsiders in a village where people had known each other for years, and Tommy's Asperger's alienated him from the cliques of kids who'd grown up together."

At the mention of Tommy's name, Fred's ears perked up, and he looked hopefully at Helen and then at the door.

"Tommy's joined a science club, and my personalized baking business has helped me to get to know people. There are more smiles and greetings instead of blank stares when I walk down the street."

"With your talents in the kitchen, I'm not surprised word has gotten around about your cooking."

"Thanks, Kelly." She washed and wiped her hands on a towel, covered an assortment of cheeses with plastic wrap, and put them in the refrigerator.

"The Sentinels will be here shortly. A friend of Mary's, Amy Winter, who goes by the name Summer, asked to meet with them."

"I'll put water and snacks in the conference room. They've had a long day."

"Good idea," I said.

"Daniel's bringing Tommy home. He and Allie helped set up this morning, so they get to leave as soon as the event ends."

As if on cue, I heard crunching gravel and saw Daniel's faded blue Volkswagen bus through the window of the back door.

Before I could say more, the door burst open, and Fred and Tommy ran toward each other. He hugged the thick-necked hound around the neck while the dog bounced up and down, taking the boy for a mini pogo-stick ride.

Daniel walked in, followed by Allie. "Anyone here interested in Daniel's famous triple hot chocolate?"

Tommy shouted, "Yes!" from over Fred's head, and Allie clapped, adding a "yippee" for good measure.

Daniel headed for the kitchen. Helen moved the tray she was preparing for the Sentinels over to the side of the granite counter, giving him room to work.

He opened the refrigerator and took out a carton of milk. He poured some into a pot and started the stove. Opening a cabinet, he pulled out an unmarked plastic container, placed it on the counter, took off the top, and got a spoon from a drawer.

I leaned over and saw bits and pieces of chocolate.

Daniel put a heaping spoonful into each of the mugs he'd taken down from the cupboard. "When Helen chops chocolate for her baking, she saves the leftover pieces for hot chocolate."

"Smart." I sat on a stool next to the counter. "I placed the produce order this morning for both our places." We'd been looking for ways to consolidate our efforts, and I'd taken on ordering the fresh fruit.

"Thanks," Daniel said as he retrieved a container of cocoa from a shelf.

I watched as he added steaming milk, put the finishing touches on his creations, and took them to the kids, who'd pulled the beanbags in front of the television. Oohs and ahhs of great satisfaction followed. A chew bone for Fred elicited a happy groan. The rich, sweet smell of chocolate permeated the air.

Daniel returned to the kitchen and began cleaning the dishes. "Kelly, with us sharing duties, maybe you don't need to hire someone to replace me here."

As he bent down to put the milk carton away, a lock of hair fell across his face, and he tucked it behind his ear. It fell across his brow again as he bent over the sink. He gave me a sheepish grin. "I'll be glad when my hair grows a little longer and I can pull it back into a ponytail."

When he'd applied for the position of manager of Ridley House, he'd cut off his long hair, and his friends had helped him to put together a suit of sorts.

"You've decided to grow it back, then."

"Yes. After hiring me, Michael said it was fine to have the ponytail. He actually encouraged it, saying it was part of my heritage." He wiped the pot with a towel and put it away. "And he said a Redwood Cove suit consisted of nice jeans, a shirt, and a fleece. I was happy to comply with that!"

"I like the casualness too."

"Back to not hiring someone. I can do some of the upkeep, and I've put together a crew for Ridley House. Our needs are very similar, and they can work at both places." He shot a sideways glance at me. "This is like a second home to me. I want to continue to be part of Redwood Cove B and B."

"I feel you and Allie are part of the inn's family as well. It would seem pretty empty without the two of you here on a regular basis. I'm definitely up for giving it a try."

His wide grin spoke more than any words could have.

"I'm going to put my things away and check the conference room." I departed.

I paused a moment before opening the door to my quarters. This was another time when I still had my breath taken away. As I stepped in, a gray juvenile seagull drifted by the glass wall on my right. A lighter gray one floated in the air in the picture window in front of me. It was an amazing experience of the outdoors being inside. Relatives of the flowers on the porch added an artist's array of colors. But nothing could outshine the dazzling Pacific Ocean, the rugged rocky coastline, and the crashing waves spewing foam framed in the window.

My boss had wondered why I'd chosen to be here permanently instead of taking the executive position that would've had me visiting fabulous resorts around the world. It was simple. Nothing could beat this—being in this place and knowing these people. I treasured the Wyoming family ranch but had wanted something of my own. And I'd found it.

I took off my heavy company fleece and put on a lightweight vest. I checked my reflection in the mirror and decided it was time for a hair clip to control the mass of red waves. The moist ocean air and my naturally curly hair provided me with an ongoing perm.

I went to the meeting room and paused at the entrance. A plaque attached to the door proclaimed it to be the Silver Sentinels' Room. I turned on the lights and turned up the heater. My timing was good as I heard familiar voices from the work area.

The group filed in, followed by Helen with a platter of food. She'd already placed a pitcher of water, glasses, and plates on the sideboard. Mary placed a dog carrier shaped like a purse on the chair next to the one she'd chosen. Everyone helped themselves to refreshments and settled in at the table. Shortly after everyone was seated, Helen escorted Summer into the room.

Summer's face had even less color than it had had earlier, and her hands clutched the tortured shawl around her shoulders.

Mary bustled up to her. "Summer." She gave her a hug. "We're here to help you in any way we can."

Summer collapsed into a chair. "I'll ... I'll pay you, like I said."

"Nonsense," Gertie said as she placed food and water in front of Summer. "Drink some of this. You'll feel better. And eat something. You need your strength if you're dealing with a difficult situation."

Summer took a small sip, put the glass down, and pushed it away.

"I need to find two people." Her hands rested on her lap, limp and motionless. She stared at them and then began to wring them. "I must find them."

We all waited, letting her go on at her own pace.

"Their names are Ken Nelsen and Diane Morgan. I met them on June third, nineteen sixty-seven." She stopped talking.

That was it? Two names of people she met almost fifty years ago?

"Well, honey," Mary said, then paused. "Is there anything more you can tell us?"

Summer's lips formed a tight, straight line. She shook her head.

The Professor leaned forward. "How about what they looked like?"

Summer relaxed into the chair a bit. "It was a long time ago. I don't know if it'll help. He had sandy brown hair and wasn't on the lean side. She ... I remember the classic high cheekbones and dark brown hair cascading down her back. She was the same height as he was." She looked at me. "Probably about your size."

I was five feet six.

The Sentinels were taking notes.

"Do you know anything about their families? Where they lived?" asked the Professor.

Summer looked at her hands and stilled them. "She paid for everything. He made references to Fort Baxter, which is about forty miles from here." She turned her face away. "They smoked dope, a lot of it. They were living the hippie life. Drifting, high ... not caring."

"Can you tell us why you want to find them?" Mary's gentle voice made it an invitation, not a demand.

"No." Summer didn't offer any explanation. Her eyes were wide and her lips clamped.

That was all? What did we know? The names of two people. Vague pieces of information about their lifestyle, outdated descriptions, and an exact date of when she'd first seen them.

Her son might not have any dark secrets from the past, but maybe Summer did.

Chapter 4

"Thank you for helping me . . . and not asking for more information," Summer said.

"Honey, we've known you for years," Mary said. "You have your reasons for what you're doing, and they're just that, your reasons. We'll get on it right away."

Summer rose and stumbled a bit as she moved toward the door. Ivan immediately stood and put his hand under her arm to steady her.

"Summer, I'm happy to give you a ride home," I said.

"Thank you, but I'll be fine. My son is waiting for my call. He'll come and get me."

The Professor closed the notepad he'd been writing in. "We'll contact you as soon as we learn anything."

Ivan slowly released her, watching to be sure she was okay. With a wan smile at the group, Summer departed.

"Well, not quite a needle in a haystack, but close to it," the Professor said.

"Ha! I know that one," Ivan exclaimed. "Means hard to find. Ivan been studying idiot . . . idioms."

The group shared a laugh, remembering Ivan struggling with what he called idiotgrams. It had all started with someone mentioning that a situation was as clear as mud and Ivan wanting to know where he could see clear mud.

Mary unzipped the mesh top on the carrier next to her and folded it back. Up popped the Chihuahua's head. "I need to get Princess home and feed her."

The little dog stood up, put her feet on the edge of the opening, and blinked rapidly a few times. Mary rubbed the top of her head.

"It's close to dinnertime for all of us," Gertie said. "I made a big stew last night. Wanted to use the rest of the vegetables I'd picked from my garden. Why don't you all come over with your laptops, and we'll work at my place."

Nods and yeses indicated agreement from the group. Michael Corrigan had purchased all of them computers as a thank-you for helping out in the last investigation they'd been involved in.

Gertie stood. "Kelly, can you join us?"

"I'll pass. I want to mingle with the guests, and I have paperwork to do."

"Right, then," the Professor said. "We'll keep you informed of anything we learn."

Mary said, "Down, Princess."

The small dog dropped into her mobile home, and Mary zipped the top of the carrier closed.

"Before I forget, I want to invite all of you over Wednesday afternoon at one. I'm going to have one of my auction parties."

"Ah, fair Mary, what have you got your eye on this time?" Rudy asked.

Mary gave him one of her dimpled grins. "No, I'm not going to tell. That'll spoil the fun. You'll have to wait and see."

"What's an auction party?" I asked.

"I have an account with Terry's Auction House. It's one of the ways I find additions for my porcelain collection. I can't wait to show it to you. I have pieces of Lladró, Franz, and a number of others."

Intrigued, I asked, "How does it work?"

"You watch the auction live on the computer. You can bid via the Internet or arrange to have someone call you when your item comes up. They act as your representative. That's how I do it because sometimes there can be a problem with the connection."

"Yah," Ivan said. "Mary make special popcorn—caramel chocolate. Auction make good show like movies when people want same item."

"We've seen quite the bidding wars," Gertie added.

I said I'd be there, and the group filed out. I went to the parlor. Guests were relaxing in front of the fireplace. A couple playing backgammon asked me about local dining options, and I recommended the restaurants I knew about. I hadn't been there long enough to have personal knowledge of an extensive list. That would require some fun homework.

Returning to my room, I took out leftovers from the night before and put them in the microwave. The commercial-grade coffeemaker brought an amused smile to my face. My boss had his quirks, and one of them was the best coffee possible.

The oven beeped. I took my food and a bottle of Pellegrino to the sitting area and placed it on the coffee table. After dinner, I checked my e-mail and found one from Scott Thompson, an executive administrator for Resorts International, saying he'd arrive later in the week. Scott had decided to accept Corrigan's offer to develop a piece of property outside of town into a community center. Currently it was a company retreat and one of Michael's residences.

This would be a change for Scott. He'd traveled extensively growing up and had found a perfect fit with Resorts International, going to exotic locations for short periods of time to help in a variety of situations. He'd be in the area for at least two months—longer than his usual assignments—and Redwood Cove certainly wasn't the bustling place he was accustomed to. It'd be interesting to see how he felt about it.

I was glad he was giving it a try. Or at least I thought I was. A bitter divorce with a clichéd plot—best friend steals husband—had left me unwilling to get involved again. Scott and I had only worked together under emergency situations. This would be a chance to get to know each other under different circumstances.

Polite, thoughtful, helpful, caring . . . words that described Scott. Shaking my head to stop the thoughts, I shied away from the tug at my heart. I wanted to take each step carefully, like a horse on a precarious trail. One slip could cause disaster, and I didn't want to go down an emotional precipice again.

I got ready for bed and checked e-mail messages one last time. The Sentinels thought they'd found the man. He was a very successful car salesman who owned a number of large dealerships in towns north of Redwood Cove. The Professor had attached a picture of a heavyset man with thinning, light brown hair, a blond woman with her arm wrapped around his, and four adults standing behind them. The caption gave their names and identified them as the Nelsen family.

The message said the woman Summer sought was proving more difficult to locate, and they planned to meet tomorrow at Gertie's.

I wondered what the people meant to Summer as I turned off the light.

* * *

The next couple of days flew by. The Sentinels contacted me Sunday with the name and photo of the woman. Because she'd been married and changed her name, she'd been much harder to find. A photo of a society function showed a striking woman with a stylish short haircut. The caption said, "Diane Purcelli hosts the annual fund-raiser for San Francisco animal rescue groups." The Sentinels had given Summer the information.

Tuesday afternoon, Mary called and said Summer wanted to meet again in the morning. I checked, and the conference room was open. We made plans for getting together at ten-thirty.

The morning of the meeting, Helen and I put out refreshments and finished reviewing some notes for an event on Sunday, the annual Wine and Flowers festival held at Redwood Cove Botanical Gardens. Inns were hosting a table with information about events throughout the year. Two people manned the table in shifts of one hour. I would be paired with a local, since I wasn't familiar with the activities. I'd help with refreshments as well as get educated.

The Sentinels arrived early and got their notepads out.

Mary put a container of chocolate bars in the center of the table. "I'd like feedback on this new recipe. It uses mint chips as well as chocolate chunks."

The Professor took one and said, "Well, if you insist, my dear." The twinkle in his eyes belied any notion that he was being pressured into taking the treat.

Summer arrived a short time later and dropped into a chair. "Hello. Thank you for being willing to meet again."

The few days hadn't done anything to improve Summer's appearance. Her ghost-white face, with the dark, sunken areas under her eyes, added a zombie-like touch. I poured her a glass of water. Her hand trembled so much I was glad I hadn't filled it to the top.

She stared at us. We stared back. It was amazing how long a minute filled with silence and looks could be.

"Thank you for finding the two people," Summer finally said, breaking the silence. "I sent them registered letters. I have a signed postal receipt from both but haven't heard from them. I asked them to contact me." She stopped.

We all nodded, encouraging her to continue.

"I must talk to them . . . I must. It's a matter of life and death." Tears filled her eyes. "During the fortune telling with Auntie on Saturday, she saw the *mati*." She looked at us with a dread-filled face. "The evil eye. She said someone would die."

"Summer, is this all about a fortune you were told?" Gertie's voice sounded like a teacher's ruler hitting the desk to get the students' attention. "That's poppycock!"

"You don't understand. My son has a rare disease. He will die if he can't find a donor. What Auntie said made me realize I had to do something quickly. These people can save him."

"Can't you give him what he needs?" Mary asked.

"No. I told him I couldn't because of the medicine I take. But that's not the truth." She clenched her hands together tightly, the knuckles whitening as the bone pushed against the skin. "It's been a lie. My whole life with him has been a lie. I'm not his mother."

Chapter 5

"At least not his biological mother. I've loved him as a mother every minute of his life."

No one said anything. We waited for her to go on.

Like a dam breaking, tears flooded down her cheeks. "He doesn't know. I meant to tell him when the right time came, but it never did. I may lose him forever when he finds out."

Meant to. The phrase of regret.

"Nonsense," Gertie said. "You *are* his mother. I still remember him in my second-grade class and how excited he was about the Mother's Day gift he made for you. At recess he went down the hall looking for every teacher he could possibly find to show it to."

Summer's tears subsided, and a weak smile appeared. "I still have it—a papier-mâché crystal ball. We had a lot of fun spinning stories about the future."

Gertie got up, gave her a hug, and handed her a tissue.

"The people I asked you to find are his real parents. The woman, Diane, gave birth to him on their wedding night. Auntie acted as the midwife, and I assisted. After a couple of days and nights of crying, Diane didn't want anything to do with him. Said it wasn't what she'd thought it would be like when she was growing up with all her dolls."

Gave up her baby because he wasn't like her dolls. Wow! I took a deep breath and exhaled slowly.

"I thought he was the most beautiful baby I'd ever seen. I offered to take him, and she readily agreed. She and Ken wandered off in a cloud of marijuana smoke." She sagged into the chair. "They have what he needs to live."

"What can we do to help?" Mary asked.

"I want to get them here to Redwood Cove, talk to them, and convince them to help."

"Do you have any ideas on how to do that?" I asked.

Summer looked at me. "I want to offer them a place to stay here in town. Tell them someone wants to thank them for a present they gave her many years ago. Her gift in return is three nights' lodging. Given my son's condition, it needs to be as soon as possible." She looked at me hopefully. "This weekend?"

"We're booked right now," I said. "The festival has filled most of the places in Redwood Cove."

"Isn't there anything you can do? I'll give them tickets for the event as well."

"We've been converting four rooms over the garage and work shed into guest quarters, and they're close to ready. We've been waiting on some hardware for the doors and cabinets. There might be a chance we can make it work."

"Kelly, please. Please help me."

Her desperate tone tugged at my heart. "I'll make a few calls and see if the shipment can be rushed or arrangements made to pick it up."

"I'll pay for their stay in advance. Just let me know how much."

"We hadn't planned on renting the rooms out this weekend. I'll just charge you for the additional cleaning service."

"His parents . . . will you call them for me?" Her quavering voice made me doubt she could handle the conversations.

"If I can provide the rooms, I'll call them for you."

"Don't tell them who I am. Since they've received the letters and haven't gotten in touch with me, I'm scared they won't come."

"Okay. I'll do my best," I said.

Summer asked us to be with her if Ken and Diane agreed to come. We set one o'clock on Friday as the time and decided we would get together the next morning at ten-thirty to decide what to say. I went back to my living quarters.

A few phone calls and some obliging customer service reps and plans were made for special shipments of the hardware. They'd arrive Friday morning. I did a quick check with Daniel, and he assured me he knew some people who could do the installation. I let Summer and the Sentinels know the rooms would be ready and then thought about calling Mark's biological parents. It was such short notice. What kind of explanation could I give?

Wanting to thank someone for something from almost fifty years ago sounded like putting one's affairs in order. Generally, people took that to mean preparing in case of death, but literally it just meant good planning. It didn't mean I'd be telling a lie if I said Summer was doing that, but it would add a sense of urgency to the situation.

I looked at the information and the photos the Sentinels had given me. If everyone in Ken's family came, it'd take the four rooms. Diane Purcelli could have my room, and I had a few thoughts on how I could work something else out for myself.

I called Diane's number and left a message on her answering machine. I dialed the man's number.

"Ken Nelsen here, your trustworthy source for buying a quality new or preowned car. What can I do for you?" His strung-together words sounded like a television commercial on high speed, the speaker aware that every second had dollar signs attached to it.

"Hello. My name is Kelly Jackson. I'm manager at the Redwood Cove Bed-and-Breakfast in Mendocino County. I've been asked by a woman in the area to contact you. You gave her something many years ago, and she wants to repay you for the gift. She's providing you and your immediate family an opportunity to stay at the inn for three nights."

"What'd I give her?"

"I don't know. She wants to meet you and tell you herself."

"Well . . ."

I pressed on. "It's for this weekend. She's aware it's short notice, but she's . . . putting her affairs in order."

"Oh. I see. Sort of tying up of loose ends."

"She's also providing tickets to Wine and Flowers."

His voice perked up. "That's pricey. Always wanted to go. Lots of fancy eats and expensive wine." He paused. "Sounds like a good deal, and I'm never one to pass up something like that."

"So you'll be able to make it?"

"You said my family. I'll need four rooms."

"The place you'll be staying in has the requisite number of rooms as well as a common dining and sitting area. The woman wanting to see you would like to meet at one o'clock on Friday."

"I'll check with the others and get back to you. I certainly wouldn't want to deprive someone of a chance to thank me for a gift I gave her—you know, an act of kindness I did for her. It's only right to take her up on the rooms and the tickets."

An act of kindness. Right. I thought "free" played a big role in his decision. "I look forward to hearing from you."

The phone rang about ten minutes later.

"Redwood Cove Bed-and-Breakfast."

"Ken Nelsen here. How early can we check in on Friday?"

"There'll be no one staying there the night before as you'll be the first guests in this new addition. You can have access to the rooms at eleven a.m."

"Uh . . . you said the woman was putting her affairs in order. What if something happens to her, you know, like maybe she kicks the bucket before Friday?" His voice took on a bold, belligerent tone. "Do we still get the rooms and the tickets?"

My face heated as he spoke, and my nails dug into my palms. I wanted to reach through the phone line, put a rope around his neck, drag him through it, and put my face in his.

"I don't want us driving all the way up there and—"

Rude or not, I couldn't take any more of him. "You'll get your rooms and your tickets."

"Well, just needed to be sure."

I heard an intake of breath on the other end of the line and spoke before he could utter another word. "If you have any other questions, please don't hesitate to call. We'll have the rooms ready Friday at eleven." I hung up. There would be no customary "It was a pleasure speaking with you."

The phone rang again. What if it was Ken? I didn't want to talk to him, but I had to answer. It could be someone else. I took a few really deep breaths.

"Redwood Cove Bed-and-Breakfast. How can I help you?"

"My name is Diane Purcelli. You left a message earlier, and I'm returning your call."

Her soft voice and clearly enunciated words cooled my anger like a Wyoming breeze on a spring day. My breathing slowed, and my hand relaxed. I'd been gripping the receiver like I was holding on to a recalcitrant mule. I explained the offer to her.

"I don't need a place to stay. I have a second home in Redwood Cove." She paused. "Is the woman Amy Winter?"

I wasn't about to lie. "Yes."

"Is this about . . . her son?"

I wondered if she'd been about to say "my son."

"Yes, it's about Mark."

"I'll be there."

I gave her the time of the meeting, and we said our good-byes. Thank goodness the calls were over. Off to Mary's auction party! I hadn't been to Mary's home before, and I looked forward to seeing it. Everywhere in town was close, so it took only a few minutes to get there. I parked in front and saw the Professor's classic gold Mercedes Benz pull in behind me. Ivan and Rudy walked toward me on the boardwalk.

Mary's yard was a delightful riot of color. Red geraniums interspersed with sweet alyssum and intense blue lobelia spilled from flowerpots attached to the window. Their perfumed scent delighted the senses. Pink daises lining the walkway nodded their heads in the light ocean wind. A miniature Snow White, a red ribbon in her hair and wearing a long yellow skirt, viewed her entourage of seven dwarfs nestled among plants behind a white picket fence.

I got out as the others converged on the yard, Gertie walking next to the Professor, cane in hand. I arrived at the door first and heard a dog barking, but it wasn't the sound of an annoyed animal or one protecting its turf.

It was more than that. I knew it well. I recognized the fierce, guttural sound. I'd heard it on the ranch when our dogs confronted a predator. Everyone within hearing would hit the ground running to protect our dogs and livestock.

It was a savage sound from deep within the animal. It meant kill or be killed.

Chapter 6

I knocked on the door and got no answer. The growls grew louder and fiercer. I pounded on the door. "Mary," I yelled. "Open up." I tried the handle, but it was locked. I turned to the others, who'd started up the walk. "It sounds like Princess, and I think she's attacking something—or someone."

"Get the key," shouted Gertie.

"Where is it?" I looked around and wondered where she would hide a spare.

I didn't need to think any further. Rudy shoved Grumpy the dwarf over, grabbed a key, and tossed it to Ivan with the smooth precision developed between brothers during years of childhood practice.

Ivan pushed past me. We all crowded behind him as he opened the door.

I saw Princess attached to a denim-clad leg. A wall blocked our view of the person it belonged to. The appendage kicked out, and the Chihuahua lost her grip and skittered across the floor.

"Stop!" roared Ivan. He and Rudy ran into the room and around the corner of the wall. Ivan's strength was something to be reckoned with, but fast he and his brother were not.

The rest of us headed to a sheet-covered object thrashing around on the floor.

"Help," came a muffled cry.

We'd taken only a couple of steps when Princess stopped us, teeth bared, body rigid, and legs splayed. Her eyes shifted from one person to another. I slowly took off my jacket, knowing any sudden movement might set her off. As gently as possible, I tossed my fleece over the pint-sized terror, quickly swept her up, and headed to the nearby hallway. I put her down in the first room I found and jerked the top of the material back enough for her head to be exposed. I knew she could make her way out of the garment from there. I closed the door.

Gertie and the Professor had untangled Mary. Her face was flushed and her sweater askew.

"I didn't see who did it," Mary said. "Someone threw a sheet over me from behind, told me to get on the floor and not move, and said I wouldn't be hurt. Then I heard Princess growling and barking. She'd been asleep in her bed in the other room. There was a crash, and I felt pieces of something hitting my arm."

She looked at the floor covered in shards of white porcelain. "I wasn't particularly fond of that piece. A gift from an aunt. Glad the attacker had poor taste."

Rudy and Ivan returned.

"Went out the back gate. Didn't see anything," Rudy said

The Professor had walked away from the group and now returned. "I called the police. They're on their way."

"Mary, are you hurt anywhere? Do you need a doctor?" I asked.

"I feel okay. The sheet protected me from the breaking porcelain."

The sound of a siren turning off announced the arrival of the police. There was a knock on the still-open door, and the familiar face of Deputy Sheriff Stanton appeared. His grim look didn't bode well for the person responsible for the attack. He knew the Sentinels well. Gertie had been his fifth-grade teacher. He called them his crime-solving senior citizens—always with a note of fondness in his voice.

"Hello, folks. What's happened here?"

Before anyone could respond, a loud barking brought Princess back into the picture.

"My poor baby. I need to go get her." Mary started to stand up.

Poor baby? Ferocious guard dog, more like it.

Gertie and I hovered over her as the deputy sheriff put his hand under her arm and helped her up.

"Really," she huffed. "I'm fine." She was breathless but moving at a determined pace toward the dog's prison door. She opened it, and Princess bounded out and beat a happy paw dance on her legs. Mary scooped her up, and the dog showered her with kisses.

Princess smiled at us from the depth of Mary's arms. She cuddled the dog as she told Deputy Sheriff Stanton what had happened.

"We've had a string of robberies using the same method, or at least close to it." He frowned at the broken statue. "This hasn't happened before."

"Whoever it was moved one of the figures to my counter." She pointed to a tall statue of a knight holding a broadsword high over his head. "Better taste with that one. It's worth something."

The statue looked heavy and had a sharp point. It could've done some serious damage if it had fallen on Mary.

The deputy sheriff tapped his notepad with his pen. "We've dubbed the burglar the Lunch Thief because he or she always strikes at lunchtime. We think the voice is recorded. The same directions are always used, and people can't tell if it's a man or a woman. The person grabs money, purses, and jewelry and leaves. No one's been injured so far."

Thank goodness Mary wasn't the first.

"Mary, is there somewhere you can stay tonight?" Deputy Sheriff Stanton asked. "This robbery isn't quite like the others, in that the person might have been planning on hitting you with one of your figures. Until we can investigate more, I'd like you to not be on your own."

"I'm not on my own." She held up Princess. "She took care of things before."

"And the intruder will be prepared for her if he or she comes back," the officer replied.

"She can stay with me," Gertie piped up.

"No offense, Gertie, but I'd like a little more backup," Deputy Stanton said.

"Billy," she began in a stern voice.

"I know you can deliver a hard whack with your cane, but let's talk about other alternatives."

"My son, Stevie, will arrive tomorrow."

"Great. That leaves tonight," the officer replied.

"I'll be fine," Mary insisted.

Ivan and Rudy looked at each other.

"We take care of Mary. We watch tonight. Take turns outside," Ivan said.

"Absolutely not." Mary's face reddened. "It's cold out there."

Ivan's stubborn look said it all. "Love America. Is free country."

Mary shook her head. "All right then. You can stay in the guest room."

"No, no bother you," Ivan rumbled. "We do stakeout. Like police."

"I insist. It's the only way I'll allow it."

Ivan began to turn away. "No—"

"Fine," Mary countered, hands on her hips. "I'll sit outside with you. As you said, it's a free country."

A cold war of glares ensued.

Soft Mary had a tough side. She and Princess made a good team.

Rudy put his hand on his brother's arm. "I think we can protect Mary more by being inside her house."

"Good point, Rudy," the Professor said. "Since you can't watch the whole perimeter, it's better for you to be inside."

"We want to do what's best for Mary," Rudy said.

Ivan nodded. "Yah. Do what's best."

Mary touched Ivan's shoulder. "I'm sure you'll get a chance to do a stakeout on one of our other cases." The phone rang. Mary glanced at the clock. "That could be the auction house. The sales are going faster than they predicted. Quick, Rudy, open the computer top."

Rudy did as instructed.

Mary grabbed her phone. "Yes, this is she. Yes, I'm ready."

The computer screen came to life, and the face of a glazed porcelain Chihuahua, a Princess look-alike, filled the screen.

The bids went back and forth a few times, then Mary exclaimed, "Wonderful!" She looked at us. "I got it. I've been trying to find one for a long time." Mary brightened. "Terry's Auction House recorded the sales. We can have the popcorn I fixed and watch my winning bid."

Gertie and the Professor stayed with Mary while Ivan and Rudy left to get their things for the night. She was safe for the time being, with the Doblinksy brothers. I drove back to the inn, worried about Deputy Sheriff Stanton's concerns and the robber's change in pattern. Had the person meant to harm Mary, or had the figure accidentally fallen? The large one on the counter with the sword could've seriously injured her . . . maybe even killed her. Why use the first one? Stun her, then kill her? Why would someone want to hurt Mary?

The next morning, I checked my e-mail and found I'd been paired with Daniel at the display table for Wine and Flowers. It would be even more fun with him as a partner.

Helen and I again prepared the meeting room. It was a short distance from my living quarters, so I left my door open as I finished some paperwork, allowing me to hear the arrival of the Silver Sentinels. I heard the group assembling and joined them a couple of minutes before ten-thirty.

I entered the room and stopped dead in my tracks. There were two Marys. I shook my head. Was I seeing double? No, there was only one of everyone else. Princess, wearing a collar of blue jewels, sat on a chair between them. There was only one of her too.

Mary and Mary began laughing.

One of the Marys said, "Good morning, Kelly. I'd like you to meet my twin sister, Martha."

"Howdy. Glad to meet you," Martha said. Her volume came close to rivaling Ivan's.

The two were not just twins, but identical in terms of features. However, they'd clearly opted for different styles of clothing. Mary dressed in pastels and wore a soft, furry sweater. Martha had on denim jeans and a corduroy jacket. Mary's soft tones occupied the opposite side of the scale to Martha's blustery, loud voice.

"When Martha heard about the attack"—Mary shot a piercing glance at Gertie and got a placid smile in return—"she drove up from Sacramento."

"Pleased to meet you," I said. I suspected the sisters had had fun with this routine or a variation of it all their lives.

Martha suddenly bent over Princess and exclaimed, "Egad, woman, the dog's nails are neon blue. You painted them! It was bad enough I let you convince me to name her Princess; now she's wearing jewels and nail polish."

Princess lifted a lip. I couldn't tell if it was a smile, a snarl, or a smirk. She got up and climbed into Mary's lap.

The dog looked at Martha and, I swear, deliberately stretched her front legs in Martha's direction, displaying the brightly colored nails.

Mary petted her. "It's made for dogs and has all natural ingredients."

"Don't even think about putting any of that stuff on Sergeant," Martha said.

I walked over to the sideboard to get some coffee and noticed a pet carrier next to Martha.

She bent down, opened the door, and out marched a black Chihuahua in a denim vest with "service dog" embroidered on the side.

I remembered Mary telling me Princess had once been her sister's hearing-assistance dog and realized her loudness was probably the result of her hearing deficiency.

Mary put Princess on the ground. Sergeant strutted over, and they started to touch noses. Princess reminded Sergeant of his rank and the chain of command with a quick nip in his direction. She let him know she was in charge, as befitted royalty.

Gertie looked at her watch. "I wonder where Summer is. She's been punctual so far, and she's clearly upset over all of this."

Mary pulled out her cell phone. "I'll call her and find out." Mary tried one number with no luck.

"Maybe she's with Auntie for some reason," Gertie suggested.

"I'll try there." Mary selected another number. "Deputy Sheriff Stanton? I'm so sorry. I must've dialed the wrong number. I meant to call Despina Manyotis."

I could hear the deputy's voice, but I couldn't make out what he was saying.

Mary frowned then, with a swift movement, she covered her mouth with the palm of her hand, and her eyes widened. She listened for a few minutes, then said in an emotion-choked voice, "Thank you for telling me."

She looked at us, tears collecting in her eyes. "Summer and Auntie are dead."

Chapter 7

Auntie had said someone would die, and it had come to pass. Mary continued, "One of Auntie's customers found them yesterday afternoon. He says Auntie and Summer appear to have been poisoned. The police are thinking accidental deaths right now. The two had been drinking tea. One of the deputies found hemlock among some fresh herbs in Auntie's house. She dried them and made her own tea. Deputy Stanton is making a last check of the house."

Gertie sighed. "I didn't like the fortune telling part of what Auntie did. Don't believe in it. But she had an outstanding knowledge of herbal medicine. I took some classes from her. Hard to believe she'd make a mistake like that."

Mary nodded and dabbed her eyes with a tissue. "I agree, but her eyesight had been getting worse . . ."

"Poor Summer," I said. "All she wanted was the best for her son."

"It'll be a hard time for Mark," Gertie said. "I'll pay him a visit."

"Please let him know we're thinking about him," I said.

The others nodded in agreement.

"Dear friends," the Professor said, "this raises the question about how we should proceed regarding tomorrow's meeting."

I leaned back. "Ken and Diane are coming. I believe we should honor Summer's wishes and talk with them."

Rudy frowned. "We don't even know what illness Mark has."

"I don't think we need to know," I said. "We can talk with them to see if they have any willingness to communicate with him. If they do, then we can contact Mark with the information, and he can decide what he wants to do."

"You wouldn't talk to Mark first?" Mary asked.

I shook my head. "If they refuse to see him, I think it would only add to a difficult emotional time for him."

"I agree with Kelly," Gertie said. "If they won't see him, we drop the matter as far as they're concerned and see what we can do for Mark on our own."

Everyone thought this was a good plan.

"What should we say to these people, and who should do the talking?" Mary asked.

The Professor took out a notepad and began making notes. "I suggest we keep it simple and just tell them what we know and what Summer wanted. Mark has a medical condition requiring a family donor."

"They should know Mark isn't aware he's adopted," Gertie added. "Though he might be by now. There might be something about it in Summer's effects."

The Professor added to his notes. "She reached out to us for help when she hadn't heard from them after she received confirmation the letters had been received. That'll explain our presence."

"I'm happy to do the talking and discuss the purpose of the meeting since I've already had contact with them," I said.

And knew what kind of jerk Ken could be. I'd be prepared.

"Perfect." The Professor handed me his notes.

"I'd like to give the background," Mary said, "since I was close to Summer and Auntie."

"That would be nice," Gertie said.

"I think that does it," I said. "Diane knows it's about Mark, so there'll be no surprise there."

A deep frown creased Ivan's forehead. "How does mother who wanted doll instead of baby boy know?"

I told them about the exchange with Diane.

"Interesting," Gertie said. "I wonder if she's been keeping tabs on her son from a distance."

"I don't know," I replied. "She didn't say."

"Let's get together before the meeting at twelve-thirty tomorrow to go over the notes again in case someone thinks of something to add," Gertie said.

The Professor pulled some papers out of his briefcase. "I researched the Lunch Thief. Everything checked with what Deputy Sheriff Stanton told us." He spread newspaper articles out on the table. "The crook has been very active. Eighteen thefts in four weeks."

Martha reached over and slid a couple of the clippings in front of her. "This is who tried to hurt my baby sister?" she said in a booming voice.

"Martha, a few minutes behind you does *not* make me your baby sister!"

Martha grinned at her. "Does to me." Her voice echoed off the walls of the conference room.

Mary patted the back of Martha's hand. "Honey, I think your hearing aids need adjusting."

"Sorry." Her volume went down a notch. "New ones, and I'm still working with them."

I pulled some articles over and skimmed them. "Did you find anything we didn't know?"

"They've all been north of here. There hadn't been any in our area until Mary's incident. The people have all been exceptionally wealthy, so a quick grab and run could be valuable. Never on the weekend. I guess the robber works a regular Monday through Friday shift."

"The person wouldn't have gotten much from me," Mary said. "Some of my figures are the only things worth anything, and you can't really grab a bunch of those and run with them."

"So three differences—area, what could be taken from Mary, and what Stanton said about no attacks, if the person had planned on hitting Mary," Gertie said.

"That sums it up." The Professor turned to Ivan and Rudy. "How did last night go?"

"No person at night," Ivan shared.

Rudy laughed. "We had a great time watching the auction. It's amazing what people will pay for an object when they get caught up in a bidding frenzy."

"Guys, thanks for taking care of my little sister." Martha grinned at Mary.

Mary rolled her eyes.

Gertie said, "I've already got a room ready for both of you. Stevie will be here this evening. We should have quite a dog party with Princess, Sergeant, and his two beagles, Jack and Jill."

Martha reached in her purse and took out two new chew bones. Unwrapping them, she gave one to each dog. They sat next to their respective owners and eyed each other as they worked on their treats. Mary put the lid on her cookies. "I can't believe Summer and Auntie are gone or that Auntie made such a mistake."

"You know, my dear, if it wasn't an accident," the Professor said, "it means suicide or . . . someone murdered them."

We all sat up straighter at the word *murdered*.

"Well . . . well . . ." Mary seemed at a loss for words. "I just meant she knew her plants. It doesn't seem possible . . ."

"Not suicide for either of them," Gertie said. "Auntie was a devout Greek Orthodox, and Summer was committed to saving Mark."

"The process of elimination means someone killed them," Martha stated.

With her strident voice, the word *killed* leapt out. I doubted any of us wanted to go down that path, but there it was. The fork in the road. Accept that it was an accident, mourn them, and move on, or take a step toward a dark place where people took the lives of others.

"Not everyone cared for Auntie," Rudy said. "Some called her a witch."

"Respected in our country," Ivan added.

I turned to Mary. "Had anything unpleasant happened with any of Auntie's customers?"

Mary shifted uncomfortably. "There was one man, a fisherman, who yelled at her whenever he saw her. Told her to keep away and take her voodoo elsewhere. Auntie took remedies to his wife. They were really helping her. We tried to schedule those deliveries when he was out on his boat, but he surprised us by being there a few times."

"Did you help her make her deliveries?" I asked.

"Summer and I took turns. One of us always went with her." Mary sighed. "I also did her books."

"Anyone else you can think of?" the Professor asked.

Mary frowned. "There was this one woman. Summer and I were both there that day. I was entering sales information, and Summer was handling the *briki* for the fortune telling. When Auntie had a client, we stayed in the back of the kitchen to give them privacy. We heard a shout and breaking glass."

A bark from Princess interrupted her. Having finished her treat, the little dog appeared ready for some attention. Mary bent down, picked her up, and put her on her lap.

"We hurried into the front room and saw the coffee cup used for the reading shattered on the floor. The woman raged at Auntie and told her to keep it to herself. She turned to us and said we'd better not tell anyone what we'd heard or else. We assured her we hadn't heard anything, but I don't think she believed us."

Or else. That could mean many things.

"Auntie muttered something about *walk the path of deception and there will be a price to pay*," she continued.

"Do you know the other woman's name?" I asked.

"No, but I can find out. Auntie only used initials for my book-keeping, but she had a master list of names and what people wanted. She listed the homeopathic remedies they ordered and tracked their comments. She also kept a diary of the fortunes she told. Some people were regulars, and it helped them to discuss what she saw."

Sergeant decided it was his turn and patted Martha's foot. She obliged and picked him up.

"She left me instructions about where I could find them if something happened to her and what else I should do. I already know where to find the Book of Secrets."

"The Book of Secrets. That sounds intriguing. What is it?" I asked.

"A family volume handed down for hundreds of years. It has an herbal remedies and fortune telling background. I need to retrieve it and call her sisters."

Auntie.

The keeper of secrets.

Maybe someone *did* have a reason to kill Auntie.

Maybe Summer and Mary had become entangled in her web of secrecy, and someone decided they needed to be taken care of too.

Chapter 8

"You tell us name of fisherman, and we pay visit," Ivan said. "His name is Jack Smith. It was on a sign at his house where he advertised his charter boat business."

Rudy jotted it down. "It sounds familiar. We'll try to find him and strike up a conversation. Most of the fishermen meet at Barney's after they unload their catch for the day."

Mary put her hand on Rudy's arm. "Please don't say anything about me telling you," she said in a tremulous voice.

Rudy patted her hand. "We won't. We'll just see what we can learn."

The Professor put his clippings away. "I'll see if I can find out anything more about the Lunch Thief. I know a couple of the people mentioned in the newspaper articles as those who were robbed. Maybe they have something to add that didn't make it into the paper."

"I need to go home and get Auntie's information," Mary said. "I have a letter from Summer as well. I'll check with Deputy Stanton, and if it's okay, I'll go to Auntie's this afternoon. Her sisters will be coming for the Book of Secrets as soon as they know of her death."

Martha picked up Sergeant and put him in his carrier. "Mary, I won't be able to take you to the fortune teller's place. When I decided to come up, I called some friends, and we're getting together this afternoon at the house. Since I'm watching over you, I thought what could be better than to have a group there."

"I can take you," I volunteered.

Mary gathered up Princess, put her in the dog purse, and tucked a small, light blue flannel blanket around her. "Thanks, Kelly. I'll let you know what Deputy Stanton says."

The group made their way out with promises to be back at twelve-thirty the next day. I put the refreshments on a tray and took them to the kitchen. Helen was sitting at the counter, going through a notebook. Placing the dishes next to the sink, I joined her.

"Hi, Kelly." She pointed to a couple of recipes. "I've been deciding on what to make for Wine and Flowers."

Picking up her choices, I scanned them and saw butterscotch brownies and chocolate-chip cookie bars. "I'm looking forward to the event." I put the recipes down. "These sound delicious."

"I wanted something I could cut into small squares. They'll be perfect for you at the display table while you're taking care of the food and water, as well as keeping pamphlets out, while someone who knows the area can talk with visitors."

"Makes sense. I'll be able to help and learn at the same time. Daniel's my partner for the hour slot." I hesitated to tell her about the deaths, but she'd hear about them at some point. "I don't know if you heard, but Amy Winter is dead, as well as a woman known as Auntie, a fortune teller."

Helen's head jerked up from the list of supplies she'd started to write. "What happened?"

"The police think it's accidental poisoning. Amy was at the fortune teller's place having tea, and an officer found hemlock in some of her herbs."

"How awful!"

"I know." I didn't say anything to Helen about Summer's reason for meeting with the Sentinels, respecting the privacy she'd clung to for so long.

My phone alerted me to a text, and I saw a message from Mary saying she'd been given permission to go to Auntie's.

"I'm going to pick up Mary and take her on an errand. I'll be back in a bit."

I parked my Jeep in front of Mary's colorful garden. This time when I knocked, Princess barked with a someone's-here yip. I saw Mary glance through a side window.

She opened the door, holding the Chihuahua with one arm. "Come in, Kelly."

I entered, and she shut the door behind me. Martha gave a little wave from the dining room table, Sergeant in her lap.

"It'll only take me a couple of minutes to get my things. Please look around. You didn't get a chance to look at my collection with the ruckus going on yesterday." She disappeared down a hallway.

Display cabinets lined the walls, each one filled with sculptures. As I wandered down the line, I recognized themes. One had women in ball gowns, men in dress uniforms, and miniature orchestras. Leaning in, I examined one of a woman in a blue gown covered with tiny light blue bows, hair piled high, head tilted to the side, as she looked toward a handsome blond man. The detail spoke of a fine artist and many hours of work.

Mary came up next to me. "I see you found Samantha. She's one of my favorites. Her gaze seems so real. The artist did an exquisite job."

Her eyes sparkled as she shared her passion for her collection. Then the shine disappeared. "We should be leaving for Auntie's. I let her sisters know I was going to get the Book of Secrets." She turned toward her sister. "Martha, will you take care of Princess for me?"

"Sure thing." Martha looked at the Chihuahua. "Though I might take that nail polish off."

"You'll do no such thing," Mary retorted. "She's my dog now."

Martha grinned at the rise she got from her sister and went back to reading a book.

We got in my vehicle, and Mary directed me to an area on the outskirts of town. I drove down a short gravel lane lined with tall grass, with a meadow beyond, and parked in front of one of the most incredible cottages I'd ever seen.

Bright cornflower-blue shutters opened against the startling white building. The same blue adorned the front door, porch railing, and roof trim. Vines filled with trumpets of yellow flowers encircled porch posts.

"Wow!" I exclaimed. "It's beautiful."

"Auntie was born in Greece and took pride in creating a bit of her old country here." Mary picked up her purse and got out of the car. "She rarely locked her door, but Deputy Stanton told me he had done so. Luckily, I know where she hid her spare key. It's at the back door. We'll need to go around the side of the house."

I followed her down a path with a wire fence full of berry vines cascading down, covering the ground, and inching their way toward the path. The berries ranged in color from pink to reddish purple to deep blackish blue Bees buzzed around orange poppies randomly growing like someone had dropped seeds from a hole in their pocket as they wandered the glen. A jeweled hummingbird whizzed by.

Mary stopped and gazed around. "Auntie loved this place. She sat out here for hours."

"It feels almost enchanted. I half expect to see an elf or a fairy popping up in the meadow."

"With Auntie's powers and connections, anything was possible," Mary said.

"What do you think is going to happen to the cottage?" I asked.

"Auntie didn't have children, and the will she left said her sisters inherit everything. They might choose to live here and keep doing Auntie's work." She turned and continued walking. "I'll miss her."

We rounded the corner of the house. The backyard had several raised, wooden, boxed-in areas where a variety of plants grew. Mary reached under the bottom step of the porch, retrieved a key, and walked up the stairs. She unlocked the door to a glass-encased porch. A couple of chairs and a small outdoor table filled the corner on my left. The right side had a long counter with a sink and rows of round wooden rods hanging from the ceiling above it.

Mary pointed to the dowels. "Auntie grew some herbs and harvested others in the wild. She washed them, let them dry next to the sink, and then hung them in bunches. The police must've taken them all."

Mary opened the back door, and I followed her into a dim hallway. Ahead of me, Mary flipped a switch, illuminating the area. In a corner next to the door, I saw what looked like a shrine on a shelf about chest high. I stepped over to it and saw a small sculpture of Jesus. Red plastic surrounded a light approximately four inches high with an on/off switch on the side. A miniature Parthenon stood next it.

Mary had continued on, and I joined her. A kitchen was on my right, and I could see the living room through an open doorway. A parlor area straight ahead contained a table draped in dark blue fabric, covered with a white lace tablecloth. A coffee set on a tray rested on it.

Mary sighed. The deep, sad sound filled the quiet room. "Deputy Stanton said he found them at the table where Auntie read fortunes." She shook her head. "I still can't believe it."

I put my arm around her and gave her a hug.

She pulled a tissue from her purse. "It'll take me a few minutes.

Auntie hid items in different places." Mary headed down the hallway with slow steps.

It was eerie being in a room where two women had died. It felt like I wasn't alone, that they were still there. I moved away, into the living room.

Oriental rugs covered the floors. A collection of framed photos took up most of the space on the coffee table. I saw another tiny figure of the Parthenon and a circular string of light green beads painted with red flowers and gold leaves. A long tassel attached to them spread across the table. Lace and throws covered a brown couch and a chair with plump pillows.

Moving on to examine the pictures covering the wall, I saw a photo of a man in military attire wearing the traditional skirt of the Greek army. Another one showed a young woman flanked by two others with strong facial resemblances to her holding a large book. I couldn't make out the words written on it in intricate letters.

I moved back to the parlor and looked down the hallway.

Mary approached, holding two black binders. "I need to get the Book of Secrets from the pantry. I'd appreciate it if you'd help me."

Mary went to a door next to the kitchen. "Auntie had me help her with the book from time to time. Her arthritis made it difficult for her to handle it because of its size and weight."

She opened the door, revealing a small enclosure lined with shelves and filled with supplies. She went to the back. "We need to clear this shelf," she said, indicating one in the middle.

I helped her remove tissue boxes and paper towels. It only took a few minutes.

Mary pushed the back wall, and a door sprung open. "Auntie had this made many years ago when she had the house built. It's been home to the book. There's an area behind all the other shelves as well where she kept some cash and what little jewelry she had. The lower shelves were harder to reach, so she didn't use them often."

She reached in and pulled out a box, though calling it that didn't do it justice. The box was made of some kind of metal, and the cover and sides were embedded with jewels. It glowed in the faint light.

"Auntie polished the box every Sunday. Then she took the book out and looked at the inside cover, where all the keepers of it were listed, and thanked them for the safe care they'd given it. She showed me one time. It went back centuries. The front cover was full and almost all of the back. Tiny letters. Imagine people writing in it so long ago."

I ran my hand over the surface, admiring the ornate design.

"Let's take it to the kitchen." Mary shook her head. "It seems a lot lighter than I remember."

The tiny kitchen reflected the minimal space of the rest of the house. A small table with its round end folded down occupied an area under a window, looking out onto the backyard. Mary placed the box there, undid the clasp, and opened the lid.

She gasped. "Oh, no. It's gone! Who could've taken it? Summer and I were the only ones Auntie had helping her, and we were sworn to secrecy."

I looked into the empty container, as beautiful on the inside as it was on the outside.

Car doors slammed. Mary moved over to a side window.

"It's her sisters." Mary began to cry. "On top of losing their sister, they've lost their family treasure. They'll be devastated."

Before I could say anything, the door burst open. Ocean wind filled the entry. Two elderly women strode in, their black clothes swirling around them.

"I am Adrasteia, and this is Fotini," one of them said. "We are Despina's sisters and have come for the Book of Secrets."

"It's gone," cried Mary. "I don't know what happened."

They both stopped. Strands of gray hair had escaped from their black scarves and moved gently in the breeze.

"Only two of us knew where it was. One was Amy Winter, and she's dead. And me. I swear I told no one."

"I believe you," said Adrasteia. "Despina knew who to trust."

The other sister spoke. "Despina knew many things. They say she picked hemlock. She made a mistake."

The other one shook her head. "No. Not true. Despina didn't make mistakes. Someone killed her. She was murdered."

Chapter 9

Adrasteia strode into the kitchen and opened the window above the sink. "Despina's spirit will be with us for forty days. She will help us find the book."

The breeze from the backyard picked up the scent of the basil growing in a pot on the windowsill and carried it throughout the room. Adrasteia grabbed a clear, flask-shaped glass bottle filled with liquid next to the plant and removed the cap. She began sprinkling the corners of the room, top and bottom.

She looked at her sister. "Despina kept another container of holy water in her bedroom. Please get it and begin in the living room."

Fotini obligingly left to retrieve the liquid. I stood there, mesmerized by the ritual. Mary stared along with me.

Adrasteia finished the corners and turned to us. "There will be a service for Despina in three days and another one in forty to say farewell to her spirit. We will move into the house after that time."

"Will you be taking over her herbal remedy customers and fortune telling clients?" Mary asked.

"Probably. I will get in touch with them and ask if they'd like to continue with us," Adrasteia said.

"I have their contact information here, but I need to give it to Deputy Sheriff Stanton."

Fotini had entered the room with an identical glass bottle. "Maybe the police will find who killed her."

"Had Despina said anything to you about problems with clients?" I asked.

Fotini headed toward the living room. "Only about the usual unhappy people when they didn't get the fortune they wanted to hear."

Adrasteia put the cap on her bottle. "Some people expect to hear what they want because they're paying to have their fortune told. We see the truth. We tell the truth."

Mary nodded. "Auntie never held back what she saw."

"Despina had recently seen the path of deception one woman was on, and the woman had threatened her." Adrasteia moved toward the hallway. "She said to us someone asks me to see their future, and I tell them. They are upset that I have seen what they are doing, that I know their secret."

Mary turned to me. "Sounds like the woman I was telling you about."

I looked at the books Mary held. "Will you be able to figure out who she is with the information you have in those notebooks?"

"Yes. The initials can be matched with names, contact information, and the appointment times."

"Let's get back," I suggested, "so you can find her name and give the information to the police."

"Good idea."

"We will lock the house," Adrasteia said. "We want to finish sprinkling the holy water, say a prayer at Despina's shrine in the hallway, and water her plants."

We thanked the sisters and left, me with images in my head of flowing black robes, scarves of black, figures bending low and reaching high as they scattered drops of water, and striking blue shutters against a white wall. A slice of authentic Greece.

Mary stopped on the way out and replaced the key. We got in my Jeep, and I dropped Mary off, then headed back to the inn. Daniel's bus was parked in the lot, and he emerged from one of the new units. He waved, and I waited for him next to my Jeep.

"Hey, Kelly, how's it going?"

"Not so great. Did you hear about Auntie and Summer?"

Daniel frowned. "I did. Terrible news. Auntie was a medicine woman, a healer. I know many people who benefited from her homeopathic treatments. There's a reason the remedies have been around for hundreds of years."

"I met her sisters today. It sounds like they want to continue her work."

"I'm glad to hear that." Daniel opened the side door of his vehicle and put the tools he'd been carrying on the floor. "I put the finishing touches on the rooms, and they're ready to go."

"Thanks. I appreciate it."

I heard a crunching noise, glanced down the gravel driveway, and saw Tommy pedaling hard. He skidded to a stop in the parking lot, jumped off, and put his bike next to the garage.

"Hi," he said, not slowing for a minute as he raced to the back door.

I suspected there was a canine dancing for joy on the other side of it.

"We're paired at the information table for the event on Sunday," I said to Daniel. "It sounds like fun and a chance to learn about community events."

Daniel closed the Volkswagen's door. His black hair glinted in the sun. "In addition, you'll be able to sample food from many of the local restaurants and meet some of the chefs."

"There are certainly some advantages to living in a town that creates happenings to entice tourists."

He laughed. "There's one event at least every month, usually more." He opened the driver's-side door. "I'm off to pick up Allie."

I entered the workroom and almost stumbled over the pile of dog and boy rolling on the floor.

Helen shook her head and smiled at me. Turning to her son, she said, "Tommy, you and Fred need to move into the sitting area."

Tommy bounded up. "Race you, Fred."

The two sprinted for the area and were down on the rug in a heartbeat.

"In a couple of minutes I want you to start your homework. I'll make you a snack," Helen said.

Tommy hugged the chunky basset hound. "Okay, Mom."

Helen poured a glass of milk and put some chocolate-chip cookies on a plate. "Would you like some, Kelly?" She held up the container, and the rich scent of the cookies tempted me.

"I'll pass this time, but I know how great they are." They had been a wonderful introduction to my first day at the inn.

"Phil called. He'll arrive tomorrow afternoon and asked me to tell you to get your dancing shoes out."

"I wonder what he's got up his sleeve."

"He's pouring wine at the festival, and the organizers asked him to lead some line dances as part of the entertainment. Someone's going to take over his serving duties for a while so he can do that."

Philopoimen "Phil" Xanthis, a wine sommelier, supplied the wine for Redwood Cove B & B. He knew how much I enjoyed Greek line dancing, and he was an expert at it.

"Sounds like fun." I headed toward my rooms. "I'm going to work for a while. I'll handle any phone calls."

Helen nodded and put Tommy's food on the counter.

I entered my quarters, tossed my purse on the couch, and got some cold sparkling water. Turning on the computer, I responded to a few e-mails and reached for some folders as the phone rang.

"Good afternoon. Redwood Cove Bed-and-Breakfast."

"Hello, Kelly. It's Scott."

He didn't have to identify himself. I recognized Scott's voice.

My surge of happiness at the sound of it hit a rock wall of caution. I still wasn't over the emotional pain caused by the clichéd best-friend-steals-husband scenario I'd been through.

"Hi. Are you in town?" I asked.

"I'm at Corrigan's place getting settled in. Packing was a whole new thought process for me since I'm staying here for at least two months, and there's no big city nearby. My suits stayed home, and there are some new jeans to break in."

I knew he enjoyed the entertainment and lifestyle of large metropolitan areas. "Are you having second thoughts about your decision?"

"No. I'm looking forward to experiencing the village life you've told me about."

A while back he'd asked what people did for fun in a small town. We'd been at an event where there were many handmade items for sale. I responded they take up a hobby, and just for the fun of it, I suggested he might build birdhouses.

He'd thrown me for a loop when he said he'd do pot holders instead, since they were a better match with his interest in gourmet cooking. Scott as a chef hadn't entered my mind.

"So does that mean you'll take up a craft like the ones we saw at the Whale Frolic festival?" I asked, remembering the lighthearted exchange we'd had.

He laughed. "Maybe I'll make a pot holder or two to use while cooking. One thing I'm looking forward to, since I'll be here so long, is trying more new recipes and experimenting with some ideas I've had."

I imagined him in the kitchen wearing a white apron and stirring various pots. I liked the image.

"On Saturday, I'm going to the site of the Wine and Flowers festival to check out the setup. I'm going to have a table with information about what Corrigan's planning and ask for ideas from the community. Then I'll be back here in the afternoon. I'd love to have you come by and see the place."

"That's perfect. I'm going to the botanical gardens as well to see it beforehand, then I'll be free in the afternoon."

"I'd like to schedule the conference room at your inn for Sunday at five-thirty. I'm not set up here to handle meetings yet."

I checked the calendar. "It's open. I'll put you in."

"Thanks. It'll be nice to spend time together without having a murder on our minds, like the last time."

"I agree."

At least I hoped that was the case . . . that we wouldn't be dealing with a murder. Though it seemed like that was the direction we were heading.

Chapter 10

The next morning, I went to the Maritime Suite to check the new units one last time. Since there was a communal area, I'd decided the theme would be an elegant steamship of the 1800s, where groups gathered throughout the vessel. Black-and-white photos of steamers I'd found at an antiques store adorned one wall, and glasses with names and pictures of ships rested on a tray on the counter. I smiled, a warm feeling washing through me as I anticipated the fun I'd be having adding final touches to the decorating.

As I walked back to the inn, a silver Cadillac sedan with blindingly bright oversized chrome wheels pulled into a parking space in the lot. The driver shoved himself out, the slicked-back sides of his hair longer than what was on top of his head. He leaned forward, revealing a balding crown that peeked through a few meager stands of hair. The buttons on the bottom of his white shirt strained to keep his ample belly from sight. The gold chain around his neck glinted in the sunlight.

The passenger side opened, and a woman struggled her way out of the large vehicle's soft seat, her short legs stretching to reach the ground. Her blond hair was piled up on her head in a conical shape. It looked like the beehive my mom wore in her high school cheerleader picture. Her chunky jewelry swayed with her efforts to exit the auto.

A younger woman with the same light-colored hair joined her from the backseat. She wore a flowing print dress and blue leather sandals with a matching sweater.

"Welcome," I said.

Before I could say more, the man interrupted me.

"Morning, little lady. I'm Ken Nelsen, your trusted source for your new car needs."

Little lady? Did he say *little lady*? I began to silently burn inside. I walked up to him and held out my hand. "Kelly Jackson, manager of Redwood Cove Bed-and-Breakfast, a member of the Resorts International chain." I squeezed his hand a little firmer than necessary.

A flicker of surprise showed in his eyes. After we let go of our mutual clasp, he flexed his fingers tentatively and said, "Uh . . . we're here to check in."

"Right this way." I pointed to the path next to the inn that lead to the front door. I followed, giving myself some time to cool down.

We passed the flowering vines and walked up the front steps and into the parlor. I went to the oak stand where we kept the thick registration book. I flinched as the band of Ken's heavy gold watch smashed onto the top of the wooden counter. While we had the information on the computer, Resorts International liked to keep the experience of the bed-and-breakfast of old as much as possible, and we entered information by hand.

"So, what do you need from me since this is all paid for?"

"Your room and tickets for the event are covered. I need a credit card for anything else."

If he thought he was going to run up a tab for someone else to pay, he had another think coming.

He dug his wallet out and tossed a credit card next to the registration book. "This here is Sue Ellen, my wife." He flicked his hand in the direction of the older woman, then nodded at the younger woman lingering behind them, "and my daughter Edie. Daisy, my youngest, is in the car."

Sue Ellen picked up a brochure. "I've heard the new spa, Blue Water Escape, is fabulous. I'm going make an appointment." She looked at Edie. "Do you want me to make one for you?"

"No thanks, Mom. I want to do some painting and read some more before my herb class at the botanical gardens tomorrow."

Sue Ellen's liberally applied perfume merged with Ken's cologne, and the cloying sweetness obliterated the fresh air in the room, making it difficult to breathe.

Ken filled in the lines on the form I'd given him. "My son-in-law, John, will join us later. Didn't want to lose too much work time." He turned to his daughter. "Fine man, Edie. Works hard. You should be proud of him."

"I am, Dad."

"He feels like my own flesh and blood, a real chip off of the old block." He frowned. "My son, Anthony, will wander in at some point."

"Everything's ready. You'll find a complimentary basket of fruit in your rooms. Wine and cheese will be served in the parlor at four-thirty."

He gestured at the pamphlets. "Do you have any discount coupons for the place my wife's interested in or for any of those restaurants?"

I handed him a local tourist guide. "There are some in here as well as additional information about many local sites."

"Where is this one o'clock meeting I'm supposed to go to taking place?"

"It's in our conference room in this building." I pulled out a map and showed him how to get to it.

"Do you want the whole family there?"

"No, just you and your wife." I'd thought about this earlier and decided she needed to be part of the meeting since it had the potential for involving her children if Ken and Diane couldn't or wouldn't help Mark.

"I'm sure the kids will be glad to hear that. I hope it won't take long."

Three nights lodging and tickets to an expensive event, and he wanted it done and over with. He exhibited no interest in his bene-factor.

He grabbed the keys on the counter, and the women followed him out.

I walked back to the work area and could see them from the back-door window. Ken opened the trunk and took out two enormous matching suitcases, followed by a smaller version. A medium-size roll aboard and a pink flowered case followed. The young woman in the backseat of the car got out and grabbed the handle of the latter and walked toward the rooms. Her super high heels and the gravel drive-way were a dangerous combination, but she successfully wobbled her way across to the rooms. Edie took the handle of the medium-size roll aboard.

While I wanted nothing to do with the man, I felt compelled to help them. I went out the back and down to the car.

"I can help you with that," I said and grabbed the hand truck kept at the back of the deck.

"Thanks, little lady. Appreciate it," Ken said.

I was tempted to run the cart over his foot. I swung the cases onto it, their weight not a problem after a lifetime of swinging saddles onto horses. Gold letters announced their last name on the three containers. This was for three days. What did they pack for a longer trip? I hoped to never find out.

I wheeled them over to the bottom of the staircase to the steam liner rooms and pulled them off the hand truck. Sue Ellen took the small one and headed upstairs. Ken took a step after her, then looked around. I looked at the two big cases and then at Ken. My eyes locked with his. Did he expect me to carry both of them up to their rooms?

He hesitated a moment, then picked one up. "Never know what you might need. Weather here varies so much."

I picked up the remaining suitcase and went up the steps, thankful for my ranch muscles. I left them to settle in and checked the time. The Sentinels would be here in half an hour. I went into the inn's kitchen area and fixed a quick sandwich.

Helen came in from the parlor. "I saw on the board that you have a meeting at twelve-thirty with the Silver Sentinels and another at one. I've put water, coffee, and tea in the conference room, and I'll be here to check people into their rooms."

"Great. Three people will be joining us at one."

"Okay."

After lunch, I looked at e-mail, then went to the conference room at a little before twelve-thirty. Voices drifted in from the hallway. The Silver Sentinels had arrived. Mary entered, dog purse over her right arm and a container in her left hand. Martha was behind her. Sergeant peered out from the screened front of his container. The other Sentinels followed her in.

After everyone had settled, the Professor said, "Let's go over what we plan to say, then see if anyone has new information for the meeting."

We did that and found nothing to add.

"I don't have anything more for this meeting, but I have information regarding Mark. I talked with him this morning. Can you all stay after this meeting?" Mary asked

Everyone said they could. The clock on the wall showed a few minutes before one. Summer's wish to bring Mark's parents together was about to happen. As if on cue, a tall, striking woman with short salt-and-pepper hair appeared in the entrance to the room. "I'm Diane Purcelli," she stated.

"I'm glad you could make it. Thank you for coming," I said. "Please have a seat. I'm Kelly Jackson, manager of this inn."

Diane took off her black leather gloves, removed her belted coat, and carefully arranged it on the back of a chair. Her tailored gray wool pants suit accented her slender figure.

Loud voices preceded Ken and his wife. They entered the room, Sue Ellen's arm wrapped around Ken's. He disentangled himself, grabbed the nearest chair, and sat down. Sue Ellen pulled out the one next to him and seated herself.

Ken glanced at Diane, a speculative look on his face, then filled a glass of water and looked at us. "Who are all of you?" he asked. "Which one is the woman who wants to thank me for the kind thing I did for her?"

I began my explanation of the meeting. "These people are the Silver Sentinels, a group that Amy Winter, your host for the weekend, turned to for help in finding you. She sent you and Ms. Purcelli registered letters. She received confirmation they had been signed for but didn't hear from you."

Ken snorted. "I didn't receive any letter."

"My housekeeper in San Francisco told me about it," Diane said. "She forwarded it, but I haven't received the letter yet."

"She sent copies of some documents and promised not to reveal their contents to anyone if you contacted her. When that didn't happen, she turned to us for help in bringing you here," I said.

"Well, where is she? She asks us to meet with her, and she doesn't show?" Ken demanded.

I wasn't sure I was going to be able to contain my contempt. I steeled myself and said, "Amy has passed away."

Ken started to rise. "Good thing I checked with you that we'd still be covered. I guess we can go then."

I dug my nails into my palms. "We are carrying out her wishes. To get your weekend, you need to remain to hear what we have to say."

Ken sat down with a grunt.

Mary's soft voice began. "On October third, nineteen sixty-seven, you two, Diane Purcelli, then Diane Morgan, and Ken Nelsen, had a wedding ceremony. That night a baby boy was born." She looked at each in turn. "Diane was the mother, and you, Ken, the father."

Diane's face paled, and her skin turned ashen.

Sue Ellen gasped.

"Amy adopted the child and loved him as her own since the day he was born. Now a grown man, your son, Mark, is in need of some medical treatment."

"I'm going to stop you right there," Ken said. "If this is about money, forget it. An illegitimate child has no rights to what I have. He won't get anything."

Martha leaned toward Ken. "Did you and Diane get a divorce?"

Ken shot a glance at Sue Ellen, then looked at Martha. "What are you talking about?"

"I'm talking about the fact that you two were married. I performed the service. Mark is not illegitimate."

Ken's eyes darted to Sue Ellen. "That's crazy. The marriage certificate was destroyed, burned in a fire before the paperwork could be completed. I saw your file folder with the document in it go up in flames."

"It was in there, but when you two were making waves in the hot tub, I put it in my briefcase. Only my notes were in that folder."

Ken shot another look at Sue Ellen.

Martha squared her shoulders. "I do my job. Amy Winter and Despina Manyotis signed as witnesses, and I registered your marriage. Unless the two of you got a divorce, you and Diane are still husband and wife."

Chapter 11

"No way!" Ken exclaimed.

"Impossible," Diane said.

Their voices united in denial.

Martha pulled a paper from a bag she had brought with her and held up a certificate. "As I said, unless you two divorced, you're married. Your names were familiar, so I went through my files at the house and found the form."

A deep frown creased Sue Ellen's face. "How is it you conducted the service? Are you a minister or something?"

Martha put the document on the table. "I'm a captain in the Salvation Army. We're licensed to perform marriage ceremonies." She turned to Ken and Diane. "When I agree to do something, I see it through. When I couldn't find you two, I made a new certificate, had the witnesses sign, and filed it."

Ken leaned forward and slapped the table with his hand. "Hot diggity!" He looked at Diane. "That means we're married." Then he said over his shoulder to Sue Ellen, "And we're not. Let's see what your fancy divorce attorney does with that."

He turned back around to Diane with a huge grin.

The look she gave him froze any of the hot in "hot diggity."

Ken took a deep breath and leaned back. "The Summer of Love. The ceremony by the world's largest hot tub. Quite a night." His gaze rested on Diane. "I remember it well."

Her icy stare displayed no fond memories.

Ken's eyes narrowed. "And that means what is yours is ours."

A glacial chill filled the room. "Don't think for one minute you'll get your hand on one cent of my money." The freezing tones of the quietly spoken words held more power than any said in the heat of anger.

"I'm happy to help . . . Mark . . . in any way I can." Diane opened her purse and took out two cards. She rose and handed one to Martha. "Here is my contact information. My attorneys will handle the legal aspects of this situation." She nodded at the marriage certificate. "They might need to get in touch with you."

"Of course." Martha reached in her sweater pocket and pulled out a card case. She opened it and handed one to Diane. "I always keep these handy in case I run into someone in need."

Diane handed the other one to me. "I'd like to meet with you privately, if that's possible."

"Certainly." There were cards for the inn on the counter behind me. I retrieved one and wrote my personal cell phone number on the back. "Give me a call, and we'll set up a time."

Diane slipped on her coat.

Ken sat up straight and hastily pulled out a card. "Here's my contact information."

"I don't need it," Diane said and picked up her purse.

"Wait a minute. How do I get a hold of you?"

She turned to leave. "You don't."

Diane strode out of the room head high, back straight.

"This is a fine mess you've made," Sue Ellen said to Ken. "There was a reason your daddy's will left everything in trust to your legitimate children. He figured there were a few unknowns out there. But he never saw this coming. That means this person Mark gets it all, and our children get nothing."

"Now, Sue Ellen, you know that wasn't his intent. I'm sure this can be worked out."

"What do you plan on telling the kids? They're waiting in the parlor for that fun family afternoon you promised them."

Ken's face crumbled. "The kids. I forgot about them." His eyes took on a worried look, and he drummed the table with his fingers. He looked at me and cleared his throat.

"Uhh . . . would you please tell them about . . . everything? They might take it better from a stranger."

Everything? His marriage? His son? Their half brother? "That's a lot of personal information, Mr. Nelsen. Are you sure you want me to be the bearer of all that news?"

"Yes, please." He took a big swallow from a glass of water. "Please. You can tell it as an outsider. It'll have a different tone."

He had a point. There could be some strong reactions. Hearing it from strangers might help to keep emotions in check.

I gestured to the Silver Sentinels. "We all were part of Amy's request. If they're willing, I'd like them to be part of giving out the information."

"However you want to do it. I just don't want to be the one to tell them."

The Sentinels agreed, and we talked briefly about who would take what part. When we finished, Sue Ellen left to get the family. It would be the first time I'd see all of them. Edie came in on the arm of a handsome, dark-haired man dressed in a conservative navy suit and tie. I surmised it was John and, at least in terms of looks, not as much of a chip off the old block as Ken had suggested.

A slim man in a bulky gray sweatshirt and loose, worn jeans followed them in. He sat in a chair at the end of the table and crossed his legs, revealing worn sneakers and thick brown socks.

I'd only seen Daisy, their youngest daughter, from a distance. Her stiletto heels made a racket on the wooden floor as she stomped in. Her white jeans looked sprayed on. A pink, low-cut sweater with sequins scattered across the bosom, gold earrings dangling almost to her shoulders, and a silver-studded belt completed her ensemble. Her hair was in one of the disarrayed looks that took a lot of time to accomplish. She wore so much mascara I figured she'd have trouble keeping her eyes open. Daisy crossed her arms, remained standing, and fixed her gaze on the ceiling.

Ken introduced them to us. The new ones to me were his son-in-law, John Brockton, his son, Anthony, at the end of the table, and my official meeting of Daisy.

"Ken has asked us to share with you what took place in the meeting we had," I said.

Daisy put her hands on her hips. "Why can't he tell us himself? Then we can get out of here and see the town."

Ken reached up and patted her arm. "Daisy, bear with me. I asked these people to handle this. They're doing me a favor."

Daisy sighed, rolled her eyes, crossed her arms, and leaned back into the wall.

Martha began the story, and we each told our piece of it. We had decided to leave the marriage connection and the half-brother part until last. I had volunteered for that.

"The reason Amy contacted Ken is because he is Mark's father." Anthony sat up. "We have a half brother?"

I nodded. "There's more." I explained about the marriage and the certificate.

"What!" Daisy exclaimed. "Another member of the family?" She rounded on her father. "Does that mean he gets some of our money?"

"When can we meet him?" Edie asked, her face open and excited. "Of course, I'll do whatever I can to help him."

"Count me in as well," Anthony said.

Sue Ellen held up her hand. "Hold on. We have a complicated situation."

The clan turned to her.

"If your father is married to this other woman, then he's not married to me."

Shock registered on all of their faces. I could see wheels turning in Daisy's mind.

"Does that mean we're illegitimate?" Daisy's voice went up an octave. "Grandpa's will said only legitimate children could inherit."

"Daisy, we don't know what it all means right now. We'll get it squared away. We know my dad intended for all of you to have that inheritance," Ken said.

John put his hand on Ken's shoulder. "It's good timing that I've been taking more of a hand in running the dealerships. It'll give you more time to sort things out."

Anthony leaned forward. "More importantly, this man needs our help." He looked at me. "How do we get in touch with him?"

"He doesn't know about this meeting or his mother's request. At the time she wrote the letter, he didn't even know he was adopted. We didn't want to say anything to him until we knew if you would be willing to help."

"Now that we know you are," Mary said, "we'll get in touch with him. Those of you willing to help, I'll need your contact information."

Anthony got up and took one of the inn's cards, wrote a number on the back, and handed it to her. Sue Ellen took out a card and had John pass it down. Daisy looked away. That left Ken as the only other blood relative who could help. Sue Ellen and Anthony stared at him. He wiped his face with his hand, then dug a card out of his shirt pocket. He tossed it on the table and stood up.

"Let's go up to our rooms and discuss this," Ken said.

Daisy couldn't leave fast enough. She flung the door open before he'd finished the sentence. John, Edie, and Anthony followed.

Sue Ellen grabbed her coat and purse. "You have a lot of explaining to do," she muttered at him as they exited together.

I stared at the certificate on the table next to my hand. Three names. Amy Winter and Despina Manyotis ... both dead. Martha Rutledge, Mary's twin sister. I felt goose bumps form on my arms. Had the attacker been after Martha and not Mary? Who was the target? Had the plan been to kill Martha as well? And why?

Chapter 12

Gertie reached out and put her soft, thin, warm hand over mine. "Kelly, are you okay? You look as white as a ghost."

I held up the certificate. "There are three people on this. Two of them have been murdered. Mary was attacked." I turned to Martha. "But maybe they were after Martha."

"As I mentioned, I spoke to Mark," Mary said. "He found a copy of the letter Summer sent to Ken and Diane. It had a copy of his birth certificate and their marriage license."

"That means whoever received the letter meant for Ken knew the situation," Gertie said.

I stared at the document. "If the marriage and Mark's existence weren't discovered, then there wouldn't be a problem with the inheritance."

"If the witnesses were eliminated, no one would know," stated Rudy.

"Summer stressed the fact she had promised not to tell anyone if they contacted her," Gertie said.

"If they were murdered because of this information, the person figured if they acted quickly, the secret would be safe," I surmised.

"They didn't realize how desperate Summer was," Rudy said.

"Or that she turn to us for help," Ivan added.

"Money," the Professor replied. "There's a reason it's called the root of all evil."

"With this scenario, it's possible Martha was the intended victim of the attack, but they got Mary instead," I said.

The Professor had gone back to twirling his pen. "Interesting point. If someone didn't know they were twins and were using a picture, they wouldn't know which one it was."

"Someone from out of town wouldn't know there were two of us, so to speak," Mary said.

"Diane explained about her letter. Ken or someone in his family signed for his letter and knew about the marriage and the son," the Professor added.

"I think there's a bigger problem than the inheritance," I said.

They looked at me questioningly.

"The fact that they weren't divorced took the situation in a much more complicated direction," I added.

"And threatened their livelihood and made for an uncertain future in many ways," Gertie said.

Mary frowned. "It seemed that the information came as a complete surprise to both of them. How would someone find out they were still married when they didn't know it themselves?"

"If someone saw the marriage certificate," the Professor said, "it would be simple to search the Internet for divorce information—if someone thought to do that. There are numerous companies more than willing to pry into someone's life for a fee."

"Ken might have said something at some point, indicating he had no idea he'd ever been married," Rudy added. "That would make someone realize the significance of the marriage document."

"Money was certainly the foremost concern in a couple of members of that family," Gertie said.

"Now what we do?" Ivan asked.

"We need something sweet to eat that will give us strength after all of that commotion," Mary said and opened her container.

She took out a moist-looking chocolate bar, placed it on a napkin, and passed the container down. We helped ourselves. I found the sweet, rich smell of the chocolate soothing. The change of pace and the comfort food were a welcome relief from the tension we'd experienced.

Once I finished my brownie, I pulled a chart from the cabinet and posted a paper on the wall. "We have the attack on Mary. It could be random, one of a string of thefts." I jotted down "theft, random," then started a new column. "It could be related to Auntie and Amy's deaths."

Rudy said, "We know Jack Smith was angry with them. We're planning on talking to him tonight."

"We found the name of the woman who threatened us—Katrina

Costov," Mary said. "Martha and I can go through Auntie's notes and see if we can find more information and figure out where she works or lives."

I added the two names under the "Auntie/Amy/Mary" column. Then I wrote "Martha."

"You can put Ken's whole family on that list," Gertie said.

So I did.

I put the pen down. "I'll talk to them whenever I can. The only thing I know about their activities right now is that Edie plans on taking a class tomorrow morning at the botanical gardens, and Sue Ellen is planning a spa visit."

"I was thinking about taking that class," Gertie said. "I'll sign up and make it a point to sit next to her."

"Great," I said.

The Professor tapped his pencil on the table. "I'll see if I can find out anything more about our thief that would point to someone or eliminate one or more of the names on our lists. I'll also dig up as much as I can on all of Ken's family."

"Gertie, is your son still arriving tonight?" I asked.

"Yes, Stevie and his beagle crew of professional bug sniffers should be here by dinnertime. They just finished checking a hotel for bedbugs and are on their way. I'll tell him what's going on, and we'll stick together."

"Should we say anything to Deputy Sheriff Stanton?" Mary asked.

I looked at the lists. "I think it's too soon. Auntie and Amy's deaths have been officially listed as accidental. We don't have anything concrete to give him."

"Ivan and I will hopefully learn something when we talk to Jack Smith. Let's meet tomorrow afternoon and see what we have," Rudy suggested.

I checked the conference room schedule. "We can meet here at two. Will that work for everyone?"

They nodded.

Mary took Princess out of her pink purse and put her on her lap. "Mark told me Summer left him a long letter with her will, explaining everything."

"How did he take it?" Gertie asked.

"It was like you said," Mary replied. "As far as he's concerned,

Summer was his mother. No anger, no upset. Summer was his mother. Period."

"I'm glad he knows," I said. "That will make your conversation with him about Ken's family much easier."

Martha bent down and looked in on Sergeant. "Is it okay if I let him out?"

"Sure."

She opened the carrier door, and out the little black dog marched. He did a reconnaissance of the room's corners, the table's legs, and everyone's feet—a very thorough search befitting his military status.

Mary scratched Princess behind her ears. "Mark and I are going to the botanical gardens tomorrow. The manager called and wants to give Mark one of Summer's favorite plants. I'll tell him then."

The Sentinels began to gather their things.

"What did Ken mean by the world's largest hot tub?" I asked.

The Professor chuckled. "A Redwood Cove claim to fame. It's a monstrous tub built over fifty years ago. It hosted some wild parties back in the sixties. The tub was filled with dirt not long after Ken and Diane's wedding. It was damaged in the fire Ken mentioned and was considered a hazard."

"Is still there," Ivan volunteered.

Mary put Princess back into her doggie abode. "It's at the east end of State Street and is a tourist attraction now. There's a plaque with its history."

Gertie grinned. "The tub served as a local post office of sorts. There were cubby holes where people left notes for each other." Her grin widened. "I found out my students were trading their homework papers there. I went over one afternoon, gathered them all up, and left each of them notes. I had fun the next day!"

Rudy pulled on his sweater. "Drugs were sometimes traded there as well."

The Professor stood. "You should take a look at it. It's worth seeing, and your guests might enjoy learning about it."

"I'll do that. Thanks for telling me about the world's largest hot tub."

"Come on, Sergeant. Time to go," Martha called out.

The dog obliged by running into his portable crate. Martha picked him up, along with her bag.

Everyone left to begin their part in gathering information. I rolled up the chart and stowed our notes in my room. I didn't want the guests to see they were being considered as murder suspects. I went back to the conference room and put the glasses and refreshments on a tray and took it to the kitchen.

Helen looked up from the cake she was decorating. "How did the meeting go?"

"We accomplished what we had hoped for. We were able to help Summer after all."

"I'm glad to hear it."

I decided not to get into the Ken and Diane situation. I'd had my fill of their melodrama for one day. I walked over next to Helen and admired her creation. It was shaped like a horseshoe, with "Happy Birthday" on it in large green letters. Horseshoes curved around the side, making a trail like a horse walking.

"Looks like someone is in for a fun surprise," I said.

"The Hamiltons asked me to make it. They're giving their daughter a horse for her birthday." She held up a plastic toy horse. "Luckily I didn't have to make it in marzipan."

"How exciting! That's a big day in a young girl's life."

I smiled, remembering how I felt when it happened to me. Grandpa surprised me with Jezebel, my first pony. I squealed with delight when what I really wanted to do was scream with happiness. I knew better, though. I didn't want to scare her.

"My baking business has really taken off. After the Silver Sentinels posted pictures of the cake I made for Gertie's son on Facebook, the phone has been ringing off the hook. People are thrilled to be able to get something unique for their celebrations."

Helen had several hours off in the afternoon, so the timing worked out well for her new endeavor, and we happily gave her permission to use the B & B's extensive kitchen for her side job. She was new to the community, and this gave her a chance to meet the townspeople.

"I'm happy to hear it. I know how much you enjoy baking." I poured a cup of coffee from the urn on the kitchen counter. "I'm going to go to the post office. Do you need me to take anything for you?"

"No, I'm good." She went back to piping frosting and hoofprints.

I spied Fred, the basset hound, stretched out and body-blocking the back door. "Hi, Fred."

He cast a look in my direction and gave a groan of acknowledgment.

Helen laughed. "I'm convinced he can tell time. At three-fifteen, he places himself in front of the door. If Tommy comes straight home, that's when he arrives."

I went to the office, picked up the mail that needed to go out, and opened the front door. Off to the right side of the lawn, I spied Edie sitting on a chair with an easel in front of her. She had the beginnings of a painting.

Edie turned as the door opened. "Hi, Ms. Jackson."

"Please call me Kelly."

"Will do," she said and turned back to her picture in progress.

Her strokes were strong, assured. She seemed to know what she wanted on the canvas. The yard came to life as she swiped, dotted, and dabbed. A hummingbird appeared in one vegetation-filled corner. The bright blue ocean in the background provided a backdrop for her work.

"That's beautiful. How long have you been painting?"

"Thank you for the compliment." She applied a swipe of white, and the beginning of a cloud was added to the background. "Not long. Just a little over a year."

"I heard you mention you're taking a class at the botanical gardens tomorrow."

"Yes, I'm also into herbal remedies." She sighed and put her brush down. "It's terrible that Auntie is dead."

"You knew her?"

"Yes, I've taken classes from her." She sat back. "We were going start a business together."

There was a surprise. A vision of Auntie bent over in her voluminous black robes and Edie in her flowing dress flashed across my mind. Quite the contrast, to say the least. A unique pair of business partners.

"There's a restored railroad depot. It's a wonderful building. They did a fantastic job keeping the ambience. We were going to open a little shop. It's something I've wanted for a long time. A dream of mine. It'd have herbs, homeopathic remedies, and my paintings. Auntie wanted to have some charms to ward off the evil eye, the *mati,* to help people." Edie smiled. "She loved her life here, and she loved the old country. I'll miss her."

"What will happen with your business plans now?"

"I know enough that I'll go ahead on my own. I inherited money from my grandfather that I can use to fund it. My husband, John, will be more supportive of it with me handling things by myself." She tilted her head and gazed at the painting.

"What do you mean?"

"He's a shrewd businessman, and certainly knows a lot more about running an enterprise than I do. He was uncomfortable about my going into a partnership with Auntie."

"Didn't he trust her?"

"It wasn't that. John checked her out online and visited her place with me a couple of times. He was okay with her. It was the principle of it all. He was concerned about being legally tied to someone." Edie shook her head. "It's hard to believe she'd mistake hemlock for one of her herbs."

There it was again. Hard to believe. And it *was* hard to believe.

With a dreamy smile, she picked up a slender brush and began painting a deep blue flower. Her creative talent was bringing the lush garden to life on her canvas.

I said good-bye and continued on to the post office. Edie had learned what she needed to know from the Greek fortune teller. With Auntie gone, she could fulfill her goal—a business of her own. Was it something she felt so strongly about that she'd murdered to see it happen?

Chapter 13

The post office was only four blocks away. I walked on the wooden boardwalk and then onto a dirt path. There was a line when I got there. I walked past a woman in a light blue sweater and faded black jeans holding a baby. Two young boys stood behind her. One of them wore a Golden State Warriors T-shirt emblazoned with "Curry" and the number 30 under the name on the front, and played an electronic game. The younger one in a striped top finished a candy bar and shoved the wrapper in his pocket.

I went over to the supply counter and got one of the flat-rate envelopes. The two books a guest had left fit perfectly. I sealed it and took the label I'd prepared at the office out of my purse. I glanced to my right and noticed Edie's husband, John, writing on a form. His brow was creased, and he was intent on filling out the document. He didn't notice me.

The boy in the striped shirt reached for the device the other one was holding, but the boy turned away and kept playing.

The younger boy yelled, "It's my turn now. Give it to me." He grabbed for the game.

"No, it's not."

The boy in the basketball jersey held the device out of the reach of the shorter one, then ran a couple of steps away, not looking where he was going. He ran into John, and the man's pen and the paper he'd been filling out went flying.

I picked up the form and noticed it was a money order. Before I could hand it to John, he grabbed it out of my hand.

"Thanks," he said, his face flushed, and put the paper on the counter.

The boy in the Warriors shirt put the pen on the counter. "Sorry, sir."

"Boys, get over here," the woman with the baby said.

The two joined her. The one who had run away gave the game to the younger boy. "Okay. You can have it now."

An adolescent mercurial mood change.

I joined the line. John finished what he was doing and did the same. Another person stood between us. I was glad I didn't have to engage in any small talk. I'd had enough of the Nelsen family for the day.

I paid for the mailing, went outside, and paused a minute to enjoy the view. The sparkling blue sea peeked at me between rows of white buildings. Only a couple of blocks separated the post office from the Pacific Ocean, and the afternoon breeze carried its salty tang. I started to walk.

"Ms. Jackson, could I talk to you for a minute?" John called out as he exited the building.

I stopped and turned. "Sure." I noticed a bus stop bench. "Let's sit here."

"Perfect."

We settled on the wooden seat, its hard slats pressing into my back.

"It's about the paper you saw in there." He paused.

"Please. It's none of my business. You don't need to tell me anything."

His smile was a rueful one. "Actually, I feel I do. Like it or not, you've become involved in some of the dealings of our family."

That was an understatement.

"A close friend of mine has financial difficulties. I'm helping out."

"That's nice of you." But why was he telling me?

He frowned and looked toward the ocean. "Please don't say anything to my father-in-law about it. He's dead set against lending anyone money."

"I won't mention it." That was an easy request to accommodate. I planned to have as little to do with the man as possible.

"Thanks. I'm beginning to take over running the business. He recently made me a partner in two of the dealerships, and I don't want anything to mar my relationship with him."

"Why is he so against helping people?"

"He's not against helping; he's against giving them money. Ken wants people to earn it. He feels people should make their own way in the world. He and his father didn't have anything handed to them. There were some tough times among the good ones. They worked hard to build their business."

I saw an opportunity to learn more. "I know he has car dealerships. Is there more?"

John raised his eyebrows at me. "You've never heard of the Nelsen car dealerships?"

I shook my head. Clearly, I was out of touch, at least with John's world.

"They acquired a string of car businesses. It's a virtual empire now. Ken calls himself the car king. You can drive between here and the Oregon border, and there'll always be a Nelsen dealership nearby."

I decided to see what I could find out about Edie's plans and the connection with Auntie.

"Then he must be happy about Edie wanting to start her own shop."

"I guess. I don't get a business about plants and paintings, but the fact that she wants to try it says something about her desire to achieve."

"I understand you met Auntie."

"I did. Luckily Edie didn't have any interest in the fortune telling aspect of working with the woman. I didn't want her going near anything to do with that."

"I got the impression from Edie that you were reluctant to have her go into partnership with Auntie."

"Partnerships can be tricky. Even best friends find obstacles and have disagreements they don't expect." He shrugged. "That being said, I had the papers for the business drawn up, and Auntie signed them. I was going to surprise Edie next week, on our anniversary, with the forms and a lease for the shop she wanted."

"Edie feels she can do it on her own with Auntie gone."

"I know. She told me. I'll go ahead and give her the keys to the store."

He studied his hands and began turning his gold wedding band. It had a single, small diamond. "Progress on taking over the business has slowed a bit because Sue Ellen has been talking about a divorce. Edie says it's just to get attention, that she really doesn't want to end the marriage. I'm hoping with me doing more of the work, maybe they can patch things up."

I squirmed. I really didn't want to know all this personal information.

"I don't know what this new situation with the previous marriage cropping up is going to do in terms of their relationship or the business."

We saw Anthony about half a block away. He waved, and we returned the greeting. He walked toward us.

Anthony reached the bench and sat next to me. "I wanted to thank you personally, Ms. Jackson, for the work you've done on behalf of my half brother, Mark. I'm sure it wasn't easy for you and the others to carry out the wishes of someone else regarding such a delicate matter."

"We felt it was the least we could do, and it was a way to honor Summer's memory and help Mark."

"When will we know if Mark wants to meet us?" Anthony asked.

"One of the Sentinels, Mary Rutledge, is meeting with him tomorrow morning and will talk to him then. Someone will get in touch with you regarding his answer."

"Thanks." He glanced at his watch and then got up. "I've got to go. I'm meeting a friend." He smiled and left.

"I couldn't do what he does," John said. "He deals with death on a regular basis."

"What do you mean?"

"He works at a hospice house. He's a very gentle soul and has a gift for relating to people. He showed me some of the cards and letters he's gotten from the relatives of people who passed away. The gratefulness they expressed was touching."

I remembered my grandmother's slow fading. "I don't think I could do that either."

"When he's not there, he works at a homeless shelter. Besides helping with food and cleaning at the place, he counsels them as well. Anthony doesn't have a desire for material things. Ken doesn't understand him at all."

Why did this not surprise me?

"The spirit is what matters to him. He lives with the rest of the family on the estate." He laughed. "Actually, I call it the compound.

It's ostentatious, to say the least. Anthony lives over the garage, which is separate from the house. He has meals with us occasionally but goes his own way. He doesn't have to work. There's a trust for each member of the family that pays them monthly."

It was time to end learning more about this family. I started to stand. John beat me to it.

He stood abruptly. "Sorry. I seem to be rattling on. I don't often get a chance to talk about these things."

We walked the rest of the block together and said our good-byes. Then he turned and headed toward the ocean.

What kind of life must the people in that family lead? John was concerned about how Ken would react to him helping a friend in need. Actually, as I thought about it, he seemed almost fearful of what might happen.

Could this in any way relate to the deaths of Auntie and Summer? He'd indicated the marriage mess could impact the business. Did he want to take over the dealerships so much he had tried to keep the information hidden?

Chapter 14

I walked a few steps to the corner, looked at the street names, and saw I was on State Street. Looking at my watch, I thought I had time to make it to the hot tub before the evening wine and cheese. The sound of an engine caught my attention, and I looked to my right. Daniel's Volkswagen bus was headed in my direction. He stopped in front of me and leaned out the window.

"Hi, Kelly. Do you want a lift?"

"Good to see you, Daniel. I was thinking about going to see the world's largest hot tub. The Sentinels told me about it."

"Lots of stories around that tub. The Redwood Cove Museum has pictures and a couple of books about it. Hop in, and I'll take you to it."

I walked around to the passenger side and climbed in. Daniel was proud the bus was entirely original. The immaculate interior had a seat with a few age cracks here and there and the armrests were a bit frayed, but there wasn't a speck of dust.

"I ran into Rudy and Ivan, and they told me what happened this afternoon. That must've been some meeting."

"It was. Those people have a lot of sorting out to do. At least some of them are willing to help Mark."

We putted along for about four blocks, and Daniel pulled over next to a park-like area. An enormous wooden structure, faded with age, occupied the clearing. I guessed it was a little higher than my waist. Redwood trees cast a shadow over the cracked boards. The tub was surrounded by thick stands of bushes along the sides and back.

"Thanks for the ride."

"Sure thing. I'll come over to the inn a little later to pick up Allie. She and Tommy are doing their homework."

"Okay."

In front of the tub there was a wooden stand with a photograph and description protected by a plastic shield. The black-and-white picture reminded me of ones I'd seen of Coney Island. The photo showed the tub full of people. Some splashed around, and others leaned against the side. It was like a huge aboveground pool.

I began to walk around the perimeter along a well-beaten path. I looked for the hiding places Gertie had mentioned. I found a few slots here and there, and could imagine how they had been covered by a piece of wood inserted over the opening. The rim was charred in a few places.

Faded paint in what had once been psychedelic colors could still be made out on the sides. Carved initials defaced the weathered wood and marked the visits of those now long gone. The brush began to get a little thicker, but the path was still evident. I picked up my pace. I wanted to finish getting around it and go back to the inn.

I pushed past a branch and stopped. "Oh," came out on its own accord as I almost ran into two men.

I took a step back as one of them smiled, revealing rows of yellow teeth spotted with decay. His dusty, matted, dreadlocked hair had a few leaves clinging to it. His friend wore a plaid jacket with the cuffs missing. His stringy blond hair was tied back in a long ponytail. I didn't see his teeth because he wasn't smiling.

A large plastic bag rested against the leg of one of them. The other one had a duffel bag slung over his shoulder. Two more men appeared and then a third. The group uniform was one of dirty and worn.

Beyond them, two men had their backs to me, one of them holding a paper bag. The other one, in a white T-shirt, was talking to a slender, doe-eyed young man with dark curly hair who kept looking from one side to the other with rapid, jerky movements. Every so often he twitched and a spasm contorted his face. As I watched, the man with the bag passed it to the young adult.

I wanted to run, but I didn't want to turn my back on them either. I stood rooted to the ground. It seemed like I was there for minutes, but my common sense said it was only seconds.

"Ms. Jackson," Anthony's familiar voice called out.

He had been one of the two men facing away from me. He had turned and was starting toward me. My knees felt weak as relief flooded through me.

Anthony approached. "I was about to head back to your inn. Let's go together."

I nodded, fearful that anything I said would come out as a croak.

The man in the white shirt still had his back to me as he talked to the slim man, now clutching the bag. The young man's large brown eyes had taken on a wild look. I'd seen horses like that. Ready to bolt. Instead, he turned and disappeared into an opening in the brush.

Anthony and I started our circular walk around the tub, leaving the group behind.

After a few minutes, when they were out of sight and we'd put some distance between us, I stopped. "Anthony, what was that all about?"

"Well, Ms. Jackson—"

I interrupted him. "Please call me Kelly, and thank you for walking me out of there."

"They wouldn't have hurt you. I know they look scary, and it's frightening coming upon them like that. They're homeless, and they have a sleeping camp over by the old tub. There's a group that meets there nightly. When I'm in the area, I bring them what I can in terms of warm clothes, blankets, and food."

Before I could ask him any more questions, the man in the white T-shirt joined us.

Anthony nodded at him. "This is my friend Tank."

"Pleased to meet you," I said.

"Likewise," he said and extended his hand.

It was clean, and the nails were cut short. It was clear he wasn't part of the group we'd left behind. We began to walk again.

In spite of the cool afternoon, Tank wore short sleeves. At the bottom of the sleeve nearest me, the tip of a tattooed claw poked out. He didn't need a T-shirt saying Ben's Complete Gym on the front to let people know he worked out. Some men's bodies shouted exercise. He could be a model for a men's muscle magazine. The name Tank was a perfect fit.

We arrived at the intersection where we needed to turn left for the inn.

Tank stopped. "I'm off to visit some friends." He looked at me from his six-foot-plus height. "Anthony told me about what took place today. You and your friends"—the side of his mouth lifted a bit—"the

Silver Sentinels, have done a good thing." He took off in the opposite direction.

Anthony and I walked a bit in silence.

A paper bag had exchanged hands. Had I stepped into a drug deal? Had I been escorted out for my safety or because they wanted me to get away from their illicit activity?

After a couple of blocks, Anthony said, "The homeless are here for many different reasons. Some by choice, others forced by circumstances, mental illness, or addiction. I do what I can to help."

I thought about the bag. I didn't think that had anything to do with what he said he brought them. I shot him a furtive look. He said he did what he could to help. Did that mean he supplied them drugs?

We arrived back at Redwood Cove Bed-and-Breakfast. Anthony said good-bye and went up to his room. I entered the work area. Helen was busy in the kitchen off to the right. Tommy and Allie had their heads together, looking at some notes on the worktable on the left side of the room. Fred had stretched himself out under their feet.

I joined Helen. She was putting the finishing touches on a cheese tray.

I tried to put what I'd seen behind me and focus on the tasks at hand. "I'll sure be glad to call an end to this day. How are we doing with check-ins?"

Helen moved a cooling tray of muffins for tomorrow's breakfast off to the side of the counter. Blueberries spotted the sides, and their sweet aroma filled the air.

"Everyone is here," she said.

"I'll mingle with the guests for a while. Then I'm going to get some work from the office and call it a night."

"Okay," she said. "I'll put the refreshments away at six, like usual."

A fire crackled away in the open fireplace, yellow flames dancing and embers glowing. Their warmth filled the room. Their flickering shapes beckoned, "Come sit and enjoy." The fireplace had been the main source of heat for the inn when it was first built as a home for a wealthy family in the 1800s. Most of the furnishings originated from that period. What wasn't an antique was a meticulous replica. Thick wool oriental rugs covered the hardwood floors.

The goal of Resorts International was to buy historic properties, restore them, if necessary, and then preserve them. Redwood Cove had a plethora of buildings from the 1800s. Gingerbread trim, scalloped wood siding, and widow walks existed in abundance. The company currently owned three buildings in town. In addition to Redwood Cove Bed-and-Breakfast and Daniel's Ridley House, there was the imposing Redwood Heights.

I circulated among the guests, answering questions about restaurants I was familiar with and discussing the local sights. I could now add the world's largest hot tub, though I wasn't sure I wanted to mention it since the tub was a meeting place for the homeless. I was thrilled to see Ken and his family weren't partaking of the refreshments or the warmth of the fire. Their negative attitudes would only have sucked the calm and peacefulness out of the room.

Helen had placed cheese and wine in the parlor. Her artistic handwriting and cards describing the cheeses added an elegant touch. A bottle of Flying Dog merlot with a slender winged greyhound in a flowing red scarf on the label sat on a green marble wine coaster. A bottle of chardonnay rested in a chilled container.

After visiting with everyone, I went to the inn's office. I sat at the massive oak desk, admiring the wood grain and workmanship. I sorted through some folders and chose two to work on. I leaned back in the swivel chair, thought for a minute, then opened a notebook that was near at hand and began to list the information I'd learned this afternoon.

Edie wanted her dream shop. She believed John was holding back on it because of the partnership. There was a pleasant surprise in store for her, but she didn't know that now. Auntie had been a potential obstacle.

I started a new page. John had concerns that the long-ago marriage could cause some business problems. I didn't feel Diane had the slightest interest in Ken's holdings. She wanted out of the situation as fast as possible. If there was a slowdown in John taking over, it was probably temporary. And there might not be any issues.

Anthony and his paper bag were next. He worked at a hospice. Did he have access to drugs there? Was he dealing? But he didn't need money, or at least that was what I'd been led to believe. There was some question as to whether or not the "new" marriage would threaten their inheritance. Did he like being a free spirit so much that he had killed to stop the possibility of losing his income? Was he being overly helpful in supplying illegal drugs to the homeless in the belief that their needs had to be met?

Lots of questions. No answers. I'd have a lot to share with the Silver Sentinels tomorrow.

Chapter 15

I closed the notepad, put it with the folders, and headed for the kitchen with them.

Helen was wrapping the muffins for tomorrow.

"Helen, the cheese trays looked wonderful. The range of colors really set off the different types of cheeses."

"Thank you. But all I do is cut, arrange, and write the notes. Andy figures out the rest. What you commented on is his handiwork. He plans to be here tomorrow."

The cheese monger, Andy Brown, was always a delight to talk with. I learned something new every time I got together with him.

Daniel walked in the back door with an enormous pizza box. "Surprise! Friday night dinner has arrived."

Tommy and Allie jumped up, as did Fred. The trio jostled against each other as they raced for the counter.

Helen pulled plates down. "Tommy, you need to feed Fred first."

"Right. C'mon, Fred."

Fred didn't need a "c'mon." He was already at his food bowl. Tommy scooped out his dinner and put it in a ceramic dish decorated with a myriad of dogs. The basset hound's face plunged in the bowl as the kids reached for gooey slices of pizza.

I loved this new family I was becoming part of.

"Kelly, do you want some pizza?" Daniel asked.

"No, I'm calling it a night." I held up the folders and notepad. "I have work to do. A quiet evening and to bed."

Muted tones of red and blue interlaced with ivory traced their way on the hallway's oriental runner. Opening the door to my rooms, I headed for my refrigerator.

I had stocked up at the local market's prepared foods counter this morning. The items available there weren't the usual run-of-the-mill offerings. The owner made a point of buying local and organic whenever possible. This pushed creativity, on the cooking side, toward using what was available. I placed shrimp mixed with kernels of grilled corn and cherry tomatoes on a plate, along with a couple of spoonfuls of quinoa. There was a small salad of local seasonal greens.

I popped the plate in the microwave and poured a glass of cold Pellegrino. When dinner was ready, I placed it on a tray and went into the main sitting area. The food went on the coffee table, and I sank into the soft window seat with a sigh. I didn't need to watch any soap operas on television to get a full dose of melodrama. Today had provided plenty. I started to think about Ken and his family, but then firmly closed my mental door on them. I had a feeling I'd be seeing way more of them than I wanted, so they didn't need to be with me this evening.

With that, my thoughts wandered to Scott. Certainly a much more pleasant subject. I wondered why he had decided to take on the extended stay and the commitment to plan the community center. He had made it clear he loved being in places for a short time and moving on.

We enjoyed each other's company. Was it becoming more than that? I plodded with slow, heavy steps like a mule after a day of plowing when it came to thinking about a possible relationship. I shook my head. The emotional pain of my divorce had left scars. No doubt about it. And Scott said his lifestyle wasn't one to encourage a relationship. We were just good friends. He had his reasons for taking this assignment, and I doubted I was part of the equation.

I hadn't seen the property where he was staying yet. Corrigan used it for his personal visits as well as company retreats. It was a thirty-five-acre property he'd bought a number of years ago with the idea of developing it into something to give to the people of Redwood Cove. The town's isolation and small population made it difficult for certain amenities to be available to the community. It wouldn't support businesses like gyms with pools, nutritionists, and exercise coaches—services often necessary for people to lead healthy lives as long as possible.

The elderly were particularly at risk because many of them had limited mobility, and being able to drive the roads, with their twists and turns, was a challenge for those who still had their licenses. There was a shuttle service, but it was a long trip with many stops along the way to the town twenty miles north that was large enough to have a variety of businesses.

Michael had gotten to know the Silver Sentinels through the situations they'd helped with both at my inn and at Redwood Heights. As he began to make his plans, he'd enlisted their feedback. The Professor and Gertie were part of the committee that had been formed.

My boss was a generous man and thoughtful of others, as well as wealthy and powerful. Those attributes didn't always complement each other. I thanked my lucky stars once again for being given an opportunity to work for the company.

My cell phone rang. "Hello."

"Ms. Jackson, this is Diane Purcelli. I asked you about getting together earlier today."

"Yes."

"Would tomorrow morning at nine-thirty work for you?"

It was perfect because the breakfast cleanup would be done. "Sure. Where would you like to meet?"

"Let's meet at the Silver Cup. Do you know where that is?"

"I do. I've been wanting to try it."

"Exceptional coffee."

"See you then."

"And . . . thank you for what you're doing for . . . my son."

Diane had been visibly distraught when Mark was discussed. Clearly, emotions ran high for her where he was involved. It would be interesting to hear what she had to say.

I finished dinner and cleared the dishes. The work orders I'd retrieved from the office didn't take long. I picked up a book on the history of Redwood Cove I'd borrowed from the parlor. Before I could start it, my phone rang.

"Hello."

"Kelly, it's Mary. I think I know where Katrina Costov works. It's a jewelry shop on Main Street called Treasures of the Ocean."

"How did you find out?"

"Oh, you know, a call here and a call there."

I knew. She'd started the infamous phone tree that flashed through the lines, leaving them smoking once activated. They'd melt someday. I was sure of it.

"Can you go there with me at eleven?"

"That'll work. Where would you like to meet?"

"Let's meet on the porch of the Redwood Cove Museum. The shop is only about half a block from there."

"I know where that is. I'll see you there at eleven."

"Okay."

I waited for a good-bye, but it didn't come.

"Mary, is there something else?"

She cleared her throat. "I've been thinking about what happened to Auntie and Summer." Another silence. "Summer and I didn't have a set schedule when we helped with deliveries. We decided each week what days we would take. If I had made the deliveries on Wednesday, I would be the one who is dead, instead of Summer."

Now I understood all the silence. It was a difficult thought to deal with. Maybe Mary was jumping to conclusions.

"Did you always have tea with Auntie?"

"Yes, she insisted. It was a ritual. After deliveries, we sat down and had a cup of tea with a lot of sugar in it and a little bit of lemon. It was to regain our strength, Auntie said."

It sounded like Mary was right. It could've been she who died instead of Summer. Lady Luck had been her companion when the deliveries were planned. Then a prickle of excitement began. "When was the last time you saw Auntie?"

"Tuesday, the day before she died. I went with her that afternoon."

"Did she always use the same tea?"

"Yes. She had an ornate container from Greece, a family piece inherited from her parents that she kept her special blend in."

The prickle became a steady current of energy.

"If she always used the same tea, that means someone had to put the hemlock in it between the last time you saw her and when she and Summer had tea. Did she leave the house much?"

"No. Auntie was a homebody, except for when she did deliveries. She picked up what she needed when we did our rounds. These were in the early afternoon. Her hours were written on the door—closed one to three."

"Did she ever vary her routine?"

"Not even for a minute. The sign said deliveries started at one, and we left on the dot. Never five minutes after or a few minutes before."

Adrenaline coursed through my veins "That means anyone could know when she was gone, and it means the hemlock was put there Wednesday afternoon."

"Oh, my gosh, you're right, Kelly."

"This is a huge piece of information, Mary. It gives us a time frame for when the poison was placed in the tea."

"Should we tell Deputy Stanton?"

"No, not yet. We still don't have anything to prove Auntie didn't make a mistake. We're the ones thinking it's murder."

And now we knew when the killer had planted the poison.

Chapter 16

I e-mailed the other Sentinels with what we'd discovered about when the poison had been planted in Auntie's tea. They were all working on aspects of the case, and this would help them with their research. I hoped our meeting tomorrow might reveal something new about what had happened to Auntie and Summer.

We still needed to figure out if Mary or Martha was the intended target of the attack by the Lunch Thief. I felt the assault and the murders were connected. Anything we learned about one helped us with the other.

I got in bed, pulled the covers over me, and was asleep in seconds.

I rose early, raced through my routine, and headed for the kitchen. Helen was finishing the breakfast baskets as I entered. A row of them lined the counter.

"Good morning. I see we're ready to start the rounds."

Helen covered the basket she'd been working on with a red-checked napkin. "Yes. This is the last one."

"Where are Tommy and Fred?"

"It's Saturday. They both sleep in."

I laughed. "I remember how much I enjoyed that day. I had to get up very early to catch the school bus because we were so far from town. The extra sleep was a real treat. There wasn't too much of it because the stock needed tending. I could do routine things while my parents took care of animals with special needs. They made a weekend list when they knew I could help out."

"How big is the ranch?"

"It's over five thousand acres. We raise cattle and horses all year round. During the summer, it's also a dude ranch. We have quarters for paying guests and offer a variety of riding experiences."

Helen smiled. "Sounds like fun."

"Working with our customers during the summer season is what gave me my training to be able to do this job."

We decided which rooms we'd deliver to first and each took two baskets and headed off. I took the Nelsens' rooms. I wanted as few people as possible to have to come in contact with them. I deposited my first one outside Ken and Sue Ellen's room and the other one at Edie and John's. I hurried down the stairs to get to the other two, hoping I wouldn't have to see them on my return.

Lady Luck was *not* with me. Ken, in a maroon velvet robe with gold trim, was *not* what I wanted to see first thing in the morning. He was on the landing as I started up the stairs. Ken had pulled the basket's cloth back and was examining its contents. He unwrapped a muffin and sniffed it as I approached.

"Smells pretty good. Where did you buy them?" he asked.

"Everything is baked fresh on site. We have an excellent baker."

"Hmmm . . . and the coffee? What about it?"

"Regular, as you requested on your form." I figured it wouldn't hurt to remind him of what he asked for. "It's organic and comes from a local distributor. There's also the cream and sugar you requested."

"The sweets are for Sue Ellen. I like mine strong."

He winked at me like I was supposed to think a reference to strong coffee had anything to do with him.

Please let this weekend be over soon.

He took the basket into the room, and I dropped off the other two. I went down the stairs with flying feet, lest Ken appear again.

Helen and I made short work of the remaining breakfast containers and settled in for our own meal.

"The usual?" she asked.

"You bet," I replied. How could I go wrong with homemade wheat bread, chunky organic peanut butter, and locally produced berry jam?

A mound of cubed potatoes sat next to plates of chopped onions and herbs. Bacon sizzled on the stove, and a bowl of eggs was on the counter. I was surprised because Helen usually had something simple like cereal, along with Tommy.

I gestured toward the food on the counter. "It looks like you're having something different today."

She was busy putting an egg carton back in the refrigerator. "No. That's for Bill."

"Bill? I don't remember you mentioning him before. Is he someone new you've met?"

Helen's face turned crimson. "No, it's Deputy Sheriff... William... Stanton. He's one of the sponsors of Tommy's science club, and he's been working with Tommy."

"That's nice," I said.

I was at a loss for words, and that was the best I could come up with. I hadn't seen this one coming. My interactions with the sometimes-gruff officer made it hard for me to see him in this light. Now here he was, helping Tommy, and he seemed to be building a relationship with Helen.

"Daniel isn't here quite as much anymore, so it's been wonderful for Tommy to have another man in his life."

Tommy's father had passed away from cancer not long ago. Helen had taken the job at the inn to support herself and her son. She had limited marketable skills, and the opportunity to bake and help with basic chores was a good fit.

Tommy flung the back door open, Fred right on his heels.

He jumped onto a stool at the counter. "Bill's coming today to help me with the rocket I'm building, right?"

"That's correct." Helen placed his sundae-like breakfast in front of him. Layers of granola, raspberries, and yogurt made a healthy parfait.

A silver Chevrolet pickup pulled into the parking area, and Deputy Sheriff Stanton, in blue jeans and a short-sleeved tan shirt, emerged. He knocked on the back door, and Helen waved him in. He had on a black Stetson hat and brown cowboy boots. He removed his hat as he entered.

"Hi, Helen." He nodded at me, "And Ms. Jackson."

Fred planted his oversize basset hound feet on the deputy's boots, a sure way to get noticed.

"Fred." He ruffled his ears. "Thanks for the weighty welcome."

The deputy sat next to Tommy. "Do you have all the parts we need for your project?"

Tommy's head bobbed up and down. "You bet," he said around a mouthful of granola.

Helen put a plate of fried potatoes, bacon, and an omelet in front of the officer and followed it with a cup of coffee.

"This looks delicious," he said. "I'm sure it'll taste that way, too."

He took a couple of bites and turned to me. "What are the Silver Sentinels working on?"

"The usual," I replied, sidestepping the question.

He was sharp, and my fancy verbal footstep didn't work. "Do you care to tell me what that means?" He put his fork down. "It sounds like trouble."

Now what? I didn't want to discuss our activities until we had something concrete to back up what we thought.

"We're meeting this afternoon. I'll bring you up to date after that."

He frowned but went back to eating his breakfast.

I gathered my purse and put on my navy company fleece. It didn't take long to walk to the Silver Cup. Diane was entering as I arrived. She wore camel-colored wool slacks and a matching cardigan over a white blouse. The delicate notes of her perfume tickled my senses, instead of assaulting them.

"Good timing," I said.

Diane held the door for me. "Thanks for meeting with me."

"Happy to."

The fragrant smell of fresh-brewed coffee permeated the Silver Cup. I inhaled deeply several times.

We scanned the choices of exotic coffees. The names created a unique language, the intricacies known only to coffee aficionados. I ordered my usual cappuccino. Diane ordered the house blend with no cream or sugar. We spied an empty table over by the window and seated ourselves.

"You're doing a lot for me and my son. I wanted you to know my story," she began.

"That isn't necessary."

She nodded. "I know. However, if you're comfortable listening, it would make me feel better. It's been a while since I've shared it . . . a long while. My husband was the only one who knew what happened. He died three years ago."

The waitress brought our coffee. "Would you like some water?"

We both said we would, and she left to get it.

"I was only eighteen. I didn't know what to do when I had my baby. I certainly didn't feel ready to be a mother. I rationalized that my son would be better off with Amy Winter." She sipped her coffee. "The Summer of Love. You think flowers, rainbows, dancing. There was a dark side. For me, it became the summer of regret."

I sipped my cappuccino. The smoky taste of dark-roasted coffee pleased my palate and lingered on my tongue.

"I only had access to a small part of my trust and found myself without any money. Marijuana softens the hard edges of reality. When it wore off, I found myself dirty and hungry and sharing a can of beans with two others. Their sadness seeped into my soul. Later that afternoon, their stoned smiles hid the truth, but I had seen the reality."

The waitress brought our water. A slice of lemon had been added to each of the tall glasses.

"I took off my rose-colored spectacles, so to speak, and began to see what was going on around me clearly for the first time . . . all the addiction. I knew it was time to leave."

I had more of my coffee. The smooth taste of the warm, nutty-flavored liquid provided a pleasant respite during the telling of an unhappy story.

"When my money ran out, so did Ken." She arched one of her well-shaped eyebrows. "He's a true-love kind of guy," she said drily.

Her right hand moved to the single strand of pearls around her neck. She stroked the necklace.

"I called my parents, and they came and got me. There was no yelling or shouting. They loved me. My parents understood what had happened better than I did. Teens often have a rebellious stage, and I had lived mine. It just happened to be during the sixties with its free love, drugs, and communal settings." She picked up her coffee. "My defiance was over with. Gone."

"It's wonderful your parents were so understanding."

She nodded. "The years passed, but I never forgot my son. I went to college, eventually met my wonderful husband, and had two more boys. I loved being with them, watching them grow up, playing with them. That brought the hurt home even more where Mark, my first baby, was concerned."

Her voice broke, and she took another sip of coffee.

She stopped and gazed at her drink. "After I told my husband everything, I decided it was time to do something. We bought a second home here. He helped me figure out a way to help Mark without letting him know it was from me."

"What did you do?"

"I remembered Amy saying she was alone out here and something about Auntie being her only family now. We did some research and gathered information about Amy's family. I'm guessing she was estranged from them. I sent Mark an inheritance from a fictitious aunt with no return address or phone number."

"Did you ever think about contacting him?"

"Many times. I dreamed of how the meeting would go. I'd share what had happened, how much I regretted leaving him, how I'd continued to think of him. He'd say he understood, and we'd get to know each other."

"Why didn't you get in touch with him?"

"I could also see a nightmare. He'd reject me and hate me for what I'd done. I also thought it was unfair to him and Amy to show up in their lives."

"It must have been very difficult for you."

"It was. Do you . . . do you know if he's willing to see me?"

"Mary Rutledge is with him now. They're going to talk about what he wants to do."

"At least my wondering whether or not I should contact him will be behind me. I'll have that answer."

"Do your other two sons know about Mark?"

"No, they don't, but if he wants to be part of our family, he'll be welcomed with open arms. My boys are two of the nicest individuals I know."

"Where do they live?"

"In our places in the Bay Area. We have two homes, one in San Francisco and the other one in Woodside. My son, his wife, and his two young children live in the Woodside home. They're all on vacation in Europe right now."

I hadn't felt her sons would be involved in what happened to Amy and Summer, but it was nice to know they weren't in the area, according to their mother. If they ever became suspects, it would be easy to check.

"Between my family money and the businesses my husband created, we're in good shape financially. I'm prepared to help Mark with whatever he needs." Diane finished her coffee and picked up her purse. "I work with a team of first-class attorneys. I contacted them after the meeting yesterday. They'll be calling you to get more information."

I nodded. "I'm happy to help."

"Thank you for listening. I'll be waiting to hear what Mark decides." She smiled, then walked away.

She'd had her first son in her life for many years, albeit at a distance. A major turn was about to take place in her life's path. Would she be walking it alone or with Mark?

Chapter 17

I looked out the window as I finished my cappuccino, enjoying the last sip of its foamy milk. People strolled by, occasionally glancing in. Many had the relaxed looks and contented smiles of vacationers. Across the street, I saw Tank in a black leather jacket leaning against a massive maroon motorcycle with black leather, metal-studded bags hanging over the sides. Daisy stood next to him, her head hardly reaching his shoulder. The sun reflected off the chrome parts of the bike. I thought it looked like a Harley.

I remembered when my brother Vincent had bought one. Every paycheck he put a certain amount aside to buy another piece for the bike. First, he bought chrome handlebars. The exhaust pipe followed, and then the turn signals. When he was low on funds, he bought decals for his helmet. I didn't know flames came in so many colors.

He brought each new item home and raved about it in excited detail. I tried my best to be interested and enthusiastic to share his joy. But . . . chrome turn signals? I couldn't quite manage it. I uttered the appropriate oohs and ahhs and smiled a lot.

On the other hand, if someone wanted to talk about a silver-plated headstall or a new quarter horse mare, that was another matter. I'd be absorbed in an instant. To each their own, as they say.

I put my cup down, picked up my purse, and walked out of the coffee shop. I stopped at a stand with tourist magazines. I noticed one I wasn't familiar with and started leafing through it. Sue Ellen and Ken occupied a table on the deck right outside the door. She had opted for a multilayered look and was wearing several overlapping pieces of lavender material and a chunky, gold-bead necklace.

Ken was scowling, his gaze trained across the street. I looked where he was staring and saw he was watching Daisy. Tank turned away for an instant, and I saw an emblem on the back of his jacket. I couldn't quite make it out. Maybe a lightning bolt. He loomed over petite Daisy in her pink outfit and matching high heels.

Ken looked around and noticed me. "Hey there, Ms. Jackson. If you see any deals or coupons in that magazine, let me know."

"Shall do. Did you go anywhere special last night?"

"They had a two-for-one at Lenny's Diner a ways out of town. They make a pretty darn good burger."

As Ken went on about the meal and how much money he had saved, the crunchy fries, and the waitresses in their cute retro outfits, I watched the pair across the street. Tank took a turquoise helmet with bright yellow flames out of the top box on the back of his motorcycle and handed it to Daisy. A jacket followed. As she zipped up the too-large garment, he adjusted the helmet strap.

Tank pulled out a pair of boots. Daisy shot a quick glance in her father's direction, yanked off her heels, and quickly passed them to Tank. She rammed her sockless feet into the oversized boots and pulled the attached straps over to secure them. For Daisy to be willing to be seen in those clothes must mean Tank had quite an influence on her. He put on his minimal black headgear and started the motorcycle. The roar rumbled through me, confirming it to be a Harley.

Ken glanced across the street and yelled, "Daisy. Don't you dare!"

He jumped up, knocking his chair over.

The motorcycle's engine obliterated any other sounds. There was no way either Tank or Daisy could've heard his shout. Ken was halfway across the street by the time Daisy had climbed on the back of the Harley. She grabbed Tank around the middle, and off they went. A backward glance, which didn't happen, would've revealed a purple-faced Ken.

Ken stormed back to the table, picked up his chair, and sat. "Wait until I have a chance to give her a piece of my mind."

"Ken, she's over twenty-one. Daisy can do what she wants," Sue Ellen said.

"Not as long as she's living under my roof."

The car king. The ruler of his kingdom. His way or no way.

They didn't look in my direction, and I was quite content to walk away without more conversation.

I had a little time before meeting Mary and took a walk around the block on my way to the museum. The sun had recently burned off the early-morning fog. The crisp air had the flowers standing at attention, their bright colors drawn out by the sun's rays. No brandname stores lined the boardwalk; each business was unique to Redwood Cove.

The yellow house with the white gingerbread trim that was used as a museum came into view. A woman who looked like Mary stood on the porch wearing blue jeans, a floppy straw hat, and sunglasses. I'd never seen Mary in jeans. Or was it Martha?

I walked up the steps to the front of the building. "Mary, is that you?"

"Oh, good, my disguise is working."

I didn't have the heart to tell her the only other person she looked like was her twin sister.

"I didn't want Katrina to recognize me."

"Where's Princess?"

"With Martha. Having her with me wouldn't work for being incognito. Besides, she likes ordering Sergeant around."

We started down the steps. "How did the meeting with Mark go?"

"Fine. I'll tell you about it later."

We'd reached the door to Treasures of the Ocean. A variety of pins, necklaces, and earrings made of iridescent abalone shell sparkled in the window. Pendants put together with small pieces of driftwood shaped by the endless motion of the sea hung on a rack. A colorful display of shells on a blue-velvet background added to the display.

We entered the store. A slim brunette woman stood behind a counter, deep in conversation with a man wearing a black sports jacket. He reached out and put his hand over hers. They gazed intently at each other, the look speaking of their love more than a string of words could ever do. My heart skipped a beat as I remembered when my ex and I had shared those looks. Would I ever feel that way again?

Suddenly, realizing we were there, the woman quickly pulled her hand free and hurried toward us. "How can I help you?"

"We're just admiring the jewelry," I replied.

Mary had turned away and was examining a case with her undivided attention.

The woman glanced in her direction and frowned slightly. "My name is Katrina. Please let me know if there's anything I can help you with."

"Okay," I said.

The saleswoman went back behind the counter. "Is there something you'd like to see?" she asked Mary.

Mary shook her head, didn't look up, and mumbled, "No."

We spent a few more minutes checking out the items. I found some abalone-inlaid hair clips I thought my mom would like. She had long hair but almost always wore it up because of all the cooking she did for the family and employees and the work she did with the animals.

Mary nudged my side. I took it as a "secret" signal it was time to leave.

Katrina had returned to her male friend. When I glanced over, their hands were intertwined.

I started to tell her thank you, but it was clear they were in a world of their own. Mary and I departed.

Mary moved at a fast pace away from the shop. "That was her. She's the one who threatened Auntie, Summer, and me."

"What did you say Auntie's prediction was?"

"Walk the path of deception and there will be a price to pay."

The boardwalk we were walking on changed to a dirt path. This was a common occurrence in Redwood Cove.

"What happened with Mark this morning?"

"The manager of the botanical gardens gave him a lovely plant. It was a type he knew Summer loved. Mark's going to plant it near the front door."

"How does he feel about meeting his new relatives?"

"Summer left him a lengthy letter. She encouraged him to talk with his biological mother and explained what she knew of the circumstances. Summer felt Diane was a good person at heart, just young and lost when he was born."

"It was nice of her to do that for both Diane and Mark."

"Mark made it clear his mother is Summer. He's willing to meet Diane, but he wants her to know where he stands."

"She'll respect that," I said. "What about the other members of the family?"

"After being an only child his whole life, it's hard for him to think in terms of sisters and a brother. He wants to meet them and thank them for being willing to help. Mark feels they'll just have to see how things go in terms of their relationships."

"How urgent is it that he gets treatment for his medical condition?"

"He definitely isn't as anxious as Summer was. I think Auntie's prediction and her mentioning what she called the *mati*, the evil eye, had Summer overreacting."

"Has someone called Diane or Ken's family members who were interested in helping Mark?"

"Not yet. I'll do it when we're done. What are our next steps?"

"We have our meeting this afternoon. We'll pool our knowledge and decide after that."

She took off her sunglasses and the straw hat. "Good. I'll get these jeans back to Martha."

Mary ambled off, a white-haired figure who blended into the crowd around her. I kept thinking about one of the hair clips I'd seen. I thought my mom would really like it, and it would connect her with where I was. I went back to Treasures of the Ocean.

Katrina was alone and dusting a glass case. A large man in a red plaid shirt came in right behind me. She looked up, and her eyes widened as we entered, but she wasn't focused on me.

"Matthew, hi. What brings you here?"

I turned around to look at who was behind me.

"Do I need a reason to visit my beautiful wife?" His heavy work boots thudded against the floor as he walked toward her.

Uh oh. On a path of deception, Auntie had said.

"Of course not." She vigorously cleaned the counter.

"I came by so we could have lunch together."

"Again? The second time in a week? How . . . sweet." She turned and acknowledged my presence. "You were in earlier. Is there something I can help you with?"

"Yes. I'd like to look at the abalone hair clips."

"Certainly." She gave her husband a tight smile and pulled out the tray I'd pointed to.

As I examined them, she said to her husband, "With the owner gone, remember I only have an hour off for lunch. I have to be back at one."

"That'll be enough for us to catch a quick bite."

She flashed him a minuscule smile that never reached her eyes. "Rachel will be here in a few minutes to take over for me."

I chose a long silver clasp. The shell's teal blue, purple, green, and flashes of pink swirled together with pearlescent overtones. Katrina ran my card and wrapped the present.

"Thank you," she said as she handed the package to me.

A woman entered the shop.

Katrina lifted her chin and looked at her husband. "Rachel's here. Time for lunch."

As I left the store, the rest of Auntie's prediction came back to me. *Walk the path of deception and there will be a price to pay.*

It was clear where Katrina's heart was and was not. If she worked the hours she told her husband, we could drop her as a suspect for poisoning the tea. I'd be grateful to cross Katrina off. The fewer names on the list, the better.

Chapter 18

I walked back to the inn and entered through the front entrance. I was surprised to find Sue Ellen in the parlor with a book open on the table in front of her. She turned to me, and I noted that the lavender outfit suited her creamy skin, blond hair, and light blue eyes.

"Hi," she said. "I'm waiting for Ken, and I noticed the books detailing the history of this place when we checked in." She smiled at me. "I'm a history buff."

I hadn't expected this. I'd only heard her express an interest in spas up to this point.

"Is there any era or place that you particularly enjoy?"

"No, not really. I try to learn as much as I can about this area. It makes it more interesting to educate myself about where I live and areas near it, and I like to visit places where events happened."

"Is there anything special you've found in our books?"

"The day-to-day life of people back in the eighteen hundreds was amazing. How much effort they had to put into simple chores we take for granted now. Just think about washing clothes. I toss a load in the machine, put the clothes in the dryer a while later, fold, and I'm done. Back then, if you were lucky you had a hand-cranked tub and lines to hang your clothes on. Too bad if it was rainy."

"Do you and Ken have anything planned for this afternoon?"

"We're going over to the botanical gardens. Edie's taking a class there, and we said we'd join her and John for lunch." Sue Ellen closed the book, put it back on the shelf, and turned to me. "I'm sorry you've had to get involved with our family issues."

I shrugged. "I chose to do it to help out."

"Ken and I met when I was working as a bookkeeper in one of his dealerships." Her lips pressed together. "He told me he'd never been involved with a woman enough to marry her."

I decided that silence was the best course of action.

Sue Ellen frowned. "The surprises from the past that wait for us in the present."

I wanted to get on my way. "I hope you enjoy your lunch." I started to walk away.

"Speaking of the past," Sue Ellen continued, "I found some great information at the fortune teller's place. I had an opportunity to read some of Auntie's midwife journals, and they were fascinating."

She knew Auntie? I stopped walking. She must have noticed my puzzled look.

"I know you talked with Edie and are aware they were planning to go into business together. John checked her background, and I looked at her books. We wanted to get an idea of how she handled her accounts. I was over there at the beginning of this week. What I found was a very detailed person who respected people's privacy."

I glanced out the window. Ken was descending the stairs. If I was going to find out anything, I'd have to act fast.

"Were the journals part of the bookkeeping?" I asked, confused as to how they fit in.

"Heavens, no. We began talking, and she showed me some of the books she had about Redwood Cove. I noticed a series of leather-bound volumes in the bookcase and asked about them. She told me they were her records from when she was a midwife and invited me to look at them. She kept a record of the people involved, any special circumstances, and how the birth went."

Auntie had brought Mark into the world, and his birth would've been recorded there. I wondered if Sue Ellen had found out about the marriage and the existence of a son when she was at Auntie's. I decided to stop at the cottage on my way to the gardens and see what I could find.

Ken arrived and said, "I'm ready. Let's go."

He nodded at me, and the two left.

I grabbed a quick bite to eat and headed out. I took the turn that led to Auntie's cottage. I parked in front of her place, retrieved the key from where Mary had hidden it, and went in the back, as we'd done before.

The house was silent. Dead silent. The stale air imparted a lack of life to the place.

I shivered in spite of the house being warm inside.

Despina and her sisters would want me to do this. Anything to get closer to the killer. I continued on.

In the living room, I scanned the bookcase and found a series of brown, leather-covered books labeled "midwife" with dates on their spines. The third one contained the years that included Mark's birth. I'd seen the date on the certificate. I pulled it out and began to leaf through it.

I found what Auntie had written about Mark's entrance into the world. Ken's name and Diane's were there. She had included Diane's maiden name and a brief description of the wedding and noted the time of Mark's birth. A paragraph below told of Diane's rejection of the child, Summer's adoption, and Martha's submitting the marriage certificate.

I didn't know which books Sue Ellen had read. She could have found this. It would've told her that Ken had been married and alerted her to Mark's existence. Their biggest problem was the lack of a divorce. With today's access to the Internet, if she'd thought to check, she could've found out.

Should I take the book as evidence?

Yes.

Was that me talking to myself or Despina telling me what to do?

I left quickly, locking the door and replacing the key. Where could I put the book for safekeeping? I decided to check where the spare tire was kept. I pulled up the section of floor that covered it, revealing the tire and enough room to tuck the book away. Wrapping the book with a towel, I tucked it next to the tire and pulled some blankets I kept in the back over the area as an extra precaution.

Time was getting short for me to do what I wanted to do and meet the Sentinels on time. I hurried down the highway.

A three-day weekend brought out the crowds, and the lot was almost full. I went up and down a couple of rows and finally spied an empty space. I headed for the visitors' center, passing Ken's car on the way. Daisy was in the back with the door open, bent over her phone, thumbs flying. The ride with Tank must've been a short one.

I entered the building and found a small gift shop, a place to buy tickets, and a display full of information about the gardens. The store had an eclectic offering of live plants, fake ones, the usual tourist doodads, and some creative pieces of art by local painters and craftspeople.

On the far side of the building, I noticed Sue Ellen checking out a display of earrings. I looked around for Ken and saw him in an adjacent hallway, his fingers punching away on his phone. Daughter and father, for sure.

The area dedicated to informing the guests about the garden was filled with books, photographs, and maps on the wall, detailing the different areas in the garden. The grounds bordered the Pacific Ocean and included a place called the Vista Room at the cliff's edge. A series of photos showed large topiary figures. One of them reminded me of a stuffed bear with round arms and legs. A man had positioned himself next to it so people could gauge its size. It stood well above the person's head. Another photo showed the same creature outfitted in strings of lights that created a flowing scarf and twinkling eyes.

At the ticket sales register, I walked up to a woman wearing glasses and a long-sleeved, cream-colored shirt with REDWOOD COVE BOTANICAL GARDENS on the shoulder.

"Hi. I'm Kelly Jackson, and I'm working at one of the booths tomorrow. I came over today to find my spot. This is my first time here, and I heard your place covered a lot of acres. I wanted to be sure I didn't spend too much time searching around for where I'll need to be."

"I'm Judy Hanson. Pleased to meet you. Yes, it's quite large." She put a map on the counter. "The spaces are numbered, but the table won't be put up until tomorrow morning. What's the name of your group?"

"It's Lodgings of Redwood Cove."

Judy checked a list, then bent over the garden's layout. Even though it was upside down, she had no trouble circling one area.

"You're right here." She handed me the map, then pointed to the sliding-glass doors behind her. "Head out that way, and hang a left at the end of the patio. Follow the signs for the Parade of Cartoon Characters and then for Shady Glen."

"What kind of parade is it?"

"We've created gigantic topiary figures based on cartoon characters like Winnie the Pooh, Eeyore, and Tigger, and we have a parade with them at Christmas. We decorate the figures with lots of lights. It's a favorite event for tourists and locals."

"I think I saw a picture from it on the wall."

"Yes, photos of Winnie the Pooh are over there, showing him before and after decorating. We keep the figures lined up on display in one area during the year here at the gardens. People can see how they work from the inside. It's a much smaller version of the Rose Parade."

I thanked her and followed her directions. A class was in session in a grassy area just past the patio. A man had placed a variety of potted plants on a table with placards in front of them. As I watched, I saw people begin to get up. Gertie stood next to Edie, engaged in conversation. Edie pointed one way and Gertie the other. They smiled at each other and took off in their respective directions. I'd find out what that was about later.

The lush gardens were a feast for the eyes and the senses. Blooming flowers provided bursts of a myriad of colors all in a green background, ranging from deep and dark to bright and light. Their fragrance permeated the area and occasionally mingled with the ocean's saltiness when sudden gusts of wind pushed through the trees. Bird songs filled the air, from high in the trees to peeps among the plants. The mossy path felt spongy in some places, a soft cushion for my feet. It was a magical place.

A sign that pointed to the left said, "Vista Room twenty feet." I decided to take a look. A wooden structure appeared as I rounded a corner of the path and entered a quiet glen. I opened the door and found a cabin-like interior with unpainted wood floors and walls. Picnic tables and benches took up most of the space. A fireplace occupied one corner, with wood stacked beside it. Announcements on the wall listed events and classes at the garden. It looked like a great place for people to enjoy lunch while being protected from the coastal winds.

The wall facing the ocean was all glass. I walked over, looked out, and inhaled sharply as I stepped back. A momentary sense of dizziness made me unsteady. I'd seen crashing water and craggy rocks far, far below. The building was on the edge of a sheer cliff. I thought of the California earthquakes I'd read about and decided it was time to leave.

I walked back to the original path I'd been following. On my right and down a grassy slope, a creek meandered beside me. The gentle eddies and slowly swirling water carried the occasional leaf on a circular path. Here, too, flowers shared their beauty with passersby.

I reached the beginning of the parade and recognized Winnie the Pooh from the pictures. A long-eared rabbit was next. I marveled at the size of the structure. It was probably over ten feet tall. Green leaves covered the entire animal. Its rotund body had a small round tail. The head was up, and the ears went down its back. Wheels protruded from the bottom of the figure. Wooden blocks had been placed in front of them to prevent them from moving. The next one, in the shape of a tiger, was even taller and had a note saying it was Tigger. Winnie the Pooh's buddies were there.

The last one looked like an oversized horse; then I saw the long ears. I had found Winnie's donkey friend, Eeyore. The back of the topiary animal was open, and a sign invited people to enter. Chicken wire had been used for the door. I could see the edges had been rolled under to keep the sharp ends from scratching people. Ducking down, I entered the enclosure, watching my step as a sign instructed.

On the inside, the same wire created the shape and gave the plants a form to follow. Pots of plants lined the wooden floor on each side, their tendrils grasping the metal. An explanation attached to one side explained how they pulled the vines to the outside and intertwined them with the wire. A steering wheel occupied the front, with a rectangular opening above it for looking out, and there was a place for a small engine. A note said those were stored elsewhere between parades.

I stood at the front and looked through the hole cut into the leaves. There wasn't much peripheral vision, but I was sure the parade would be a slow one and along a well-known route. Being able to see a lot wasn't a priority. Several people could fit in the beast. Fun! I was in a Trojan donkey . . . of sorts.

It got darker inside the leafy animal, and I turned. The wind must've closed the door. I went to it and pushed. Nothing happened. I noticed a latch for a handle, but it wasn't latched. Puzzled, I pushed again.

The creature began to move. How could that be? I'd seen the blocks in front of the wheels. Suddenly it picked up momentum. The wheels creaked. I could feel it start to turn right, and it began to tilt forward. It was heading toward the creek.

"Help!" I yelled.

Then I heard the voice.

"Mind your own business, or you'll have no business to mind."
The screeching wheels almost kept me from being able to hear
the words.

"Who are you? Let me out of here!" I screamed.

The only response I heard was a grunt. Then the plant vehicle
began to accelerate—downhill. I stumbled to the front and saw what
might be an emergency brake. I pulled on it, and the vehicle slowed,
but the sculpture was too heavy to stop.

The donkey, with me stuck inside, continued to race downward. I
heard a splash, and water filled the bottom of the structure. Eeyore
and I came to an abrupt halt as the wheels sank into the mud of the
bank. I took a deep breath. We were leaning downhill. Water flowed
by up to my knees, but at least we weren't moving. I began to inch
backward on the wooden floor. The donkey wobbled. I breathed
deeply and inched back some more. I felt the animal sway with the
current. I couldn't see out through the vines.

I turned carefully, crawled to the back, and began to follow the
line of the door with my fingers. It wasn't easy with all the leaves.
Something was holding it closed, and I needed to find what it was.
Partway between the handle and the top of the door, I found several
pieces of wire twisted together.

The person had uncoiled the edge and connected the chicken wire
with the edge of the door. I'd worked with the stuff on the ranch and
knew it would grab at any opportunity. The structure hadn't moved
right away. As I was turning, they must have been twisting. I hadn't
been able to see anything because it was dark and the vines had hidden the movement.

I untwisted the three strands and shoved the door.

Mistake.

The door still held, and the movement made the vehicle slip forward a little bit farther into the stream and almost go over on its side.
I grabbed at the wire. The cut ends bit into my hands. My heart
pounded with fear. If it fell over, I'd be trapped in a wire cage in the
water. I took in a deep breath.

The donkey slid forward a couple more inches. The water came
up to my thighs, and the current made the animal dance from side to
side. I willed myself to be slow and calm. I went back to examining

the door and found two more wired areas. After untwisting them, I pushed gently and felt some give. I carefully moved the door back and forth. It opened a couple of inches and then stuck in the mud because of the embankment. But it was almost enough to get through.

The creature settled a little more. I pushed again, and it began to go over on its side. As it did, the door moved upward and pulled out of the mud. I grabbed the sides and threw my body forward, landing on the door top. The wire bit into my waist. My chest was out of the water.

I brought a knee up and pushed against the frame. My body cleared, and I held on to the couple of inches of the structure that remained above the water. I swung my legs into the creek and held on to the submerged vehicle for support, trying to decide what was the best way to get to the bank. The donkey had shifted toward the center of the creek when it fell, and the water was almost at my waist.

I let go of the wire and slogged through the water toward shore. The gentle eddies hid a powerful current. The mud pulled at my feet as I neared land. I willed myself to yank each foot out as the mud tried to hold on. I reached the bank and collapsed on the ground, sucking the air deep into my lungs.

My heart raced like a spooked horse.

Kelly, you made it. You're okay.

I talked to myself as I would a frightened animal. My heart slowed.

I thought of what the person had said. *"Mind your own business, or you'll have no business to mind."*

That was clearly a threat. He—or she—had given me a chance to change my actions. Had the person decided to take it a step further? Had someone just tried to kill me?

Chapter 19

The sky was still blue. Flowers still lined the edge of the creek, and the birds were still singing.

And I had come close to drowning.

I sat up. I needed to call the police. Should it be a 911 call? The attacker could come back to see if they'd succeeded. The mythical garden creatures formed a stationary parade along the road above me. A group of children with several grown-ups began to gather around Winnie the Pooh.

"Are you all right?" a voice called out.

I looked up to my left and saw a man and a woman with two German shepherds. I had company.

I was safe.

For now.

"Yes. Thanks . . . I just slipped." I stood up to show them I was okay but almost didn't succeed in accomplishing that. I was shakier than I thought, and one ankle complained.

The man handed the leash he held to his companion. "Let me help you up. The bank is slippery."

He made his way down and supported me under my arm. I was grateful for the assistance. A small portion of Eeyore's frame showed above the creek. The man frowned and looked puzzled but didn't say anything.

I thanked the couple and hobbled over to a bench. I took out my phone and turned it on. It didn't look like the water had damaged it. A 911 call wouldn't accomplish anything. If the person was still in the area, he or she was now just another visitor. I phoned Deputy Sheriff Stanton instead.

"Ms. Jackson. How can I help you?"

No reason not to get right to it. "Deputy Stanton, someone threatened me, possibly tried to kill me."

"Are you all right?"

"A little banged up, but overall okay."

"Where are you?"

"At Redwood Cove Botanical Gardens."

"Are you alone?"

"No. Not any longer. There are quite a few people around."

"Stay with them. I'm on my way."

"Hold on," I said.

One of the adults with the children said it was time to go. They were heading back.

"There's a group going back to the entrance. I'll tag along with them."

"Okay. I'll meet you out front."

I followed along a short distance behind. The group's slow pace suited me just fine.

I went into the restroom when we got back to the patio area and thoroughly washed my hands with soap and water. There were some scratches, but none appeared to be deep. I splashed water on the mud splotches on my pants, then wiped off my shoes with wet paper towels.

My reflection in the mirror showed that my hair had dried and the natural curl had made it wavy. I wet a paper towel and wiped the few spots of dirt off my face, but there wasn't anything I could do about the dank smell of the stream. When I exited the building, Sue Ellen and Ken were having coffee at one of the wooden tables. Edie and John had joined them. I didn't see Daisy. She was probably still on her phone.

I made my way to the front entrance. As I exited, a black Mercedes drove in. I recognized the car. It belonged to Resorts International. The driver was luckier than I was and found an open spot right away. Scott got out, saw me, and waved. He headed in my direction.

I looked at my soggy pants and shoes, then at my scratched hands. I shoved them in my wet pockets, being careful not to flinch as the cloth rubbed against the cuts.

"Kelly, hi!"

How could he look elegant in faded blue jeans and a plain white shirt?

"Good to see—" He stopped talking as he took in my appearance.

"What happened to you? Are you okay?" Any lightness to his tone vanished.

My shoulders sagged. "I . . . I . . ."

The flashing lights of Stanton's patrol car heralded the arrival of the officer as he rounded the driveway and stopped next to us.

"I'll tell you later if we're still on for this afternoon," I replied.

The set of Scott's mouth was grim. "Yes, we're still on."

Stanton got out and approached me. "Ms. Jackson, let's talk in the car."

With a nod at Stanton, and a penetrating look at me, Scott left. Stanton held the passenger door open for me and then found a place to park.

"Are you okay?"

"A bit of a bruised ankle and scratched hands. That's about it."

He pulled out his notepad. "What happened?"

I described the attack.

"You said you had to pull at the wire. Please show me your hands."

I held them out, palms up.

He examined them, raised his eyebrows, and said, "Okay. I have some antibiotic ointment in the car you can put on those scratches when we get back. Are you able to walk well enough to go back and show me the location?"

I nodded. "It hurts a little, but I'll be fine."

"Let's go see the place."

I limped a bit as we walked. I appreciated the fact that he took it in stride and recognized the difference between minor and major issues.

We reached the creek. The donkey's vegetation-covered side protruded several inches above the water. Leaves attached to the structure bobbed up and down, alternately covered with water and popping into view. Stanton's somber face surveyed the scene as he took notes.

"You are right. You could've been killed. It's time for you to tell me what's been going on."

We sat on the same bench I'd occupied earlier as I told him everything I knew, what the Silver Sentinels and I had been doing, and what our suspicions were.

He shook his head. "The attack shows you're getting to someone, but we don't know for what reason. There's nothing to indicate the deaths of Auntie and Summer weren't accidental, and that's how they've been reported. I can't investigate those unless something changes the classification, but your attack will be pursued, and we'll continue to look into Mary's incident. I'll ask some questions about what you've told me regarding Auntie and Summer."

"Thanks, Deputy Stanton."

"I'll get a crew out here. We'll check the structure and the surrounding area for anything that might lead us to who is responsible, but I don't have high hopes we'll find anything." He put his notepad away. "You need to be careful until we find out what's going on."

I stood, and we began walking. "I know. No solitary walks in lonely places. I promise."

We were back at the parking lot. He pulled some ointment from his first-aid kit and handed it to me. I applied some to my cuts, and we went our separate ways. I was anxious to get back to the inn, shower, and change into clean clothes.

I parked and retrieved the journal from the wheel well. I entered through a seldom-used side door, not wanting to answer any questions about my appearance.

I cleaned up, made an espresso, and sank into the window seat. I had a few minutes before I needed to meet the Sentinels. I thought about what had happened. The screeching wheels had made so much noise, I hadn't been able to make out if the voice belonged to a man or a woman. Who could've felt so threatened that they had almost killed me? Since the attack was against me, it was someone I'd had contact with. I thought about the people I'd questioned. There was no obvious suspect.

I looked at my watch, roused myself, and gathered the chart we'd started at the last meeting. Helen, on top of things as usual, had coffee, water, and tea available in the conference room. She was good at checking the schedule and making the room ready. Sergeant was on the floor near Martha, who had her back to me as she rummaged through her purse.

"Hi, Martha."

She didn't respond. Instead, she kept digging through her bag. Sergeant had sat up when I said Martha's name. He looked at me, then at his owner. He ran to her, stood on his hind legs, and began pawing at her. She looked at him, and he did a quick circle and headed toward me. Martha turned and followed.

"Hello, Kelly." Her voice was on loudspeaker volume.

I jumped a bit, startled by the sound.

"Sorry," she said in response to my movement. "I'm having trouble adjusting to my new hearing aids and took them out." This time she'd turned her volume down and spoke at a normal decibel level. Martha walked to the chair where she'd placed her purse, picked up the devices next to it, and put them in her ears.

I looked at Sergeant, who seemed pretty pleased with himself, if his doggie smile was any indication. "Is that how Sergeant alerts you? Tapping on your leg?"

"It depends on what sound it is. He knows a variety of signals. When someone calls my name and I don't hear them, he taps, then circles around to let me know to follow him."

"It's amazing what dogs can contribute to our lives."

The Chihuahua had settled next to Martha's feet.

"To be a hearing-assistance dog, he needs to know at least three signals, but Sergeant knows more than that."

"What are some of the things he does?"

"I often take my hearing aids out when I'm home. If the phone rings and I'm sitting down, he jumps on my lap and pushes my stomach with his front paws. If I'm standing, he plants them on my legs."

Sergeant stood and wagged his tail, sensing he was the focus of our conversation.

"When he hears a knock at the door, he does what you saw today." Martha sat down. "Princess knows those commands as well, but she started getting a little hard of hearing and was missing some sounds."

Mary bustled in. "Thanks for the ride, Professor," she said over her shoulder as the gentleman followed her into the room.

"You're welcome, my dear."

Gertie came in and leaned her cane against the table. "I appreciate it, too."

The Professor smiled at her.

Mary placed her dog purse on the chair, and Princess popped into view.

Male voices with Russian accents heralded the arrival of the Doblinsky brothers.

I unrolled the chart and put it on the wall. Gertie was sitting near me as I turned around.

"Kelly, what did you do to your hands?" Gertie demanded. "Let me see."

She sounded like a teacher looking after one of her wayward kids.

I held my hands out.

Gertie said. "What happened?"

I gazed at the scratches. "Someone almost killed me today."

Chapter 20

Mary pulled a container out of the bag she'd carried in. "You need these. They're medicinal."

She pulled the lid off and put the plastic box in front of me. Inside were her signature double-fudge brownies. The scent of chocolate was a delight to inhale. Gertie poured me a cup of coffee and set it next to the treats. I reached for one of the chocolate confections. It was a perfect time for my favorite combination. I let the sweetness coat my taste buds and the caffeine seep into my body.

Finally, I began the story of what had happened, and a short while later they knew it all.

Mary nudged the container closer to me. "I'm glad you're okay. Have another brownie. It'll give you some energy."

The Professor had opened his notepad. "It shows you hit someone's nerve. We need to figure out who."

A second brownie sounded good to me, and I helped myself. "I agree, and I want to know what all of you have discovered."

I stood, went to the chart, and reviewed what we had so far. "We were trying to decide what was the impetus behind the murder of Auntie and Summer. We made our first column about Auntie's business. Was someone so angry with her that they killed her and Summer as well? Our second list concerned the attack on Mary. Was it random, possibly by the Lunch Thief, or connected to Auntie and Summer? Or was it a case of mistaken identity and Martha was the target because she was one of the three people on the marriage document? That would connect Martha to the third list, which was the possible consequences of the revelation of the long-ago marriage." I added, "Who would want to keep that from happening?" to that particular heading.

The Professor pointed to the first column. "Let's talk about threats to Auntie and Summer first."

Ivan's voice boomed, his volume close to Martha's, without her hearing aids. "We check on fisherman that not like Auntie helping wife. Big man with little heart."

Rudy leaned forward. "We shared a beer with Jack Smith last night. He hated Auntie and her potions and fortune telling, but Ivan and I felt he feared her. Jack seemed very superstitious."

"And he gone at the important time you sent us," Ivan said.

Rudy nodded. "He occasionally went to sea for a period of a couple of days. He was out on a boat on Wednesday when you determined the poison was planted."

"Good," Gertie said. "One to cross off our list."

I did the honors.

Mary picked up Princess and put her in her lap. "Katrina Costov is on that list. Today I confirmed she was the one who threatened Auntie, Summer, and me. Kelly and I went to the store where she works, Treasures of the Ocean."

I put Treasures of the Ocean after Katrina's name on our chart. "I went back to get a hair clip for my mom. She mentioned the hours she'd been keeping because the owner is gone. If she was telling the truth, she was working Wednesday afternoon and couldn't have gone to Auntie's. Someone named Rachel covered during lunch, and that was from twelve to one."

Gertie sat up straight. "Probably Rachel Harding. She works part-time at a number of different stores. I know her. She was in my fifth-grade class. I can talk to her."

I added her name after Treasures of the Ocean. "That only leaves one person threatening Auntie—Katrina—and it looks like she probably has an alibi."

Mary's attack was in the next column. All the information we had on the robber had been added, but it hadn't pointed us in any new direction.

"I haven't found anything more about the Lunch Thief that would help us," the Professor said. "I've been collecting information about Ken and Diane's families. Nothing jumps out as important, but we can add what I've learned to the chart."

The third column, which we'd labeled "issues with the marriage," had Ken and Diane's names and "inheritances of children" noted under it.

"We talked about why people would kill to keep this from being known," I said. "Money took first place. Let's discuss how that would impact the two families involved." I held up my felt pen. "Where would you like to start?"

Rudy got up and came over to me. "Let me do the writing. You've had a rough day."

I was grateful to take the weight off my ankle and let my hands have to hold only a brownie or a coffee mug.

"Let's do Diane," I said. "She's very wealthy, and I can't see any motive on her part. Even if Ken was able to claim some of it as a spouse, it wouldn't change her lifestyle. Because of the extent of her holdings, she has a group of attorneys she works with. They're top of the line, and I think they'll make mincemeat of this whole situation."

The Professor examined his notes. "What I've learned concurs with that. She's quite a philanthropist, and much of what I found out came from the society columns."

"Her husband left their two sons a very successful business, and they live on family estates," I added. "They're on vacation in Europe and have been since last week."

"I have the name of their corporation and some financial background. It corroborates what she told you," the Professor said.

Gertie said, "I suggest we forget about Diane for now and concentrate on Ken's family."

Ken's family. Money was so much the focus of their lives.

"Who should we start with?" Mary asked.

"I feel a new chart is in order just for this family," Rudy said as he wrote the name Ken on a new piece of paper he'd put on the wall. "He's the one who's responsible for the disruption to his family." He transferred the piece about the kids' inheritance being jeopardized.

I picked up my coffee cup. "His son-in-law told me he calls himself the car king."

"Kelly, is it okay to put Princess on the floor?" Mary asked. "She and Sergeant can play while we talk."

"Sure. Good idea."

Mary placed the tan Chihuahua on the floor, then dug in the bag she'd brought in with her. I hadn't had a chance to see the collar of the day yet. As Princess trotted over to her new buddy, I saw purple leather studded with matching sparkling rhinestones about a quarter inch in diameter. Sergeant had his everyday black web collar on.

Mary pulled out a long, fluffy green toy. She turned its face toward me, and I saw yellow antennae and large yellow circles with black felt pupils.

"Caterpillar?" I asked.

Mary nodded and tossed it on the floor. "Princess loves it. It's bigger than she is, but she gets the better of it!"

The two dogs each took an end and began a tug-of-war. There was a knock on the door. Ivan, closest to it, got up and opened it.

Tommy held a bowl in his hands. "Mom thought the little dogs might like some water."

"How thoughtful," I said. "Please put it at the end of the room."

Tommy did as instructed, and Princess and Sergeant followed him, carrying the toy between them.

Fred had accompanied Tommy into the room. He hadn't met the canine guests before. The two Chihuahuas dropped the stuffed animal and approached him. They sniffed his nose, as he did theirs. Their tails quivered in their version of wagging. Fred's branch-sized tail went into an overtime wag. His front end went down and his back end up. He was in play pose.

Suddenly, Fred lunged for the green caterpillar. He grabbed it in the middle and shook it. The yellow antennae wiggled up and down. Princess grabbed one end of the stuffed worm and Sergeant the other. Then Fred began to run down the length of the room, nails clattering, the little dogs holding on like water-skiers, their legs stiff, their bodies leaning back as they glided over the slick surface of the polished hardwood floor. Fred slipped a bit, so the pace wasn't very fast.

Fred turned and headed for the door, with his new friends in tow. Tommy knelt in the doorway and flung out his arms to keep him from getting out. Fred sat back on his haunches but couldn't stop his momentum on the smooth floor. He plowed into Tommy, knocking him over. Tommy laughed and grabbed him around the neck. The two little dogs decided a laughing boy on the ground was more fun than the green toy and began jumping on Tommy.

Helen appeared behind the canine chaos. "I'm so sorry your meeting got interrupted."

We were all laughing so hard we couldn't comment right away.

Mary wiped away tears from the corners of her eyes. The humor was a welcome change from the topic of our discussion—murder.

"Thank you for the water, and thank you for being the impetus for a canine comedy scene," Martha said.

Helen shook her head and rolled her eyes. "It never ends with these two. Let me know if you need anything."

"Will do," I said.

Tommy jumped up and dashed out the door, Fred on his heels. Helen closed the door behind the dynamic duo.

"All right. Let's get back to the chart and list what impact Ken's marriage to Diane could potentially have on him," the Professor said.

Gertie spoke up. "Just as he suggested that some of Diane's money was his, she could claim the same thing. The self-proclaimed royalty of car dealerships could have his kingdom threatened."

Mary put down the brownie she'd been nibbling on. "But he mentioned an impending divorce. It might help him there. The divorce might not be necessary, and that would be a good thing for him."

The Professor shook his head. "I don't think so. Sue Ellen helped to build the business. She'd have some rights to a piece of it. He could have two women going after what he owned."

Rudy wrote Sue Ellen's name next. "The wife might have the same concern about Diane taking from the business. That would mean less for her."

Gertie had been making her own notes. "We know her children's inheritances were also in jeopardy. Mothers can be very protective when they perceive threats to their children."

Mary sighed. "We're focusing on money, but there was also the potential humiliation for Sue Ellen to deal with if her husband was married to someone else. Her kids could possibly be considered illegitimate."

"Would that cause her to murder?" Rudy asked.

"Who knows," Mary said, "what's important in her life."

"I found out earlier today she might have known about Ken's marriage and his son Mark," I said.

I described what I'd found in Auntie's journal.

Gertie toyed with her pen. "All three children and the son-in-law could have the same inheritance concern, which we've already noted."

"Let's put down what we know about them as individuals," the Professor suggested.

I had the list in front of me that I'd started Friday evening. "Ken's made John a partner in two of the dealerships and planned on more. If an ownership question came into play, that would probably stop, at least for a while."

The Professor fingered the bill of his wool cap. "I found a few references to that in the paper, but there wasn't anything that seemed unusual about it."

"Edie is starting a business. She said she'll be using money from her inheritance," I said.

Sergeant patted Martha's leg, and she bent down, grabbed him, and put him in her lap. That signal had a dual purpose—to let her know when someone called her name and a request to be picked up.

"John told me Anthony lives with the family and volunteers at a homeless shelter and a hospice home."

"If that's the case," Mary said, "since he doesn't work, he'd lose his lifestyle if he lost his money."

Martha scratched Sergeant behind the ears. "I don't think that matters to him. Anthony wants to talk to me about what it's like working for the Salvation Army. We're going to get together before I go back to Sacramento. He seems a very compassionate person and wants to help others. He's ready for a change and is looking into a variety of options."

I wondered if I should I say something about the possible connection with drugs. I decided the answer was yes.

"There's an incident I haven't told you all about yet. I don't see that it has anything to do with the deaths, but it's more overall knowledge."

I told them what had transpired.

"Thanks, Kelly," Martha said. "If Anthony decides he wants to go forward with applying for a Salvation Army position, I'd like to talk to him about what you just told me. Is that okay?"

"Certainly. I'd want you to. He may have a perfectly acceptable explanation."

Martha had more to add. "He and his friend Tank helped me at the gardens today. We were roping off the parking lot for tomorrow's event. The men from the shelter help direct the cars, and the place earns a portion of the parking fees."

"Did you work together with him the whole afternoon?" I asked, thinking of the recent attack.

"No. It's a large area, and we had different tasks. Sorry, Kelly. I know it would be nice to cross someone off of the list of who might have attacked you," Martha said.

My phone rang. Stanton. "I'm going to take this," I told the group.

People got up and filled coffee cups and water glasses.

"Hello, Deputy Stanton."

"Ms. Jackson, I wanted to let you know that I stopped by Treasures of the Ocean this afternoon. Thought I'd talk to Katrina Costov. Rachel Harding was there. She said Katrina came back after lunch and said she'd had it and was leaving her husband. She asked Rachel to take her place at the shop. Rachel agreed to do it. A man drove up in a red BMW, and Katrina got in the car, and it sped off. She hightailed it out of town before that attack on you."

Katrina had made the decision.

"Rachel also confirmed that Katrina worked on Wednesday during the hours you believe the poison was planted. The store was busy, and Rachel stayed on after lunch."

"Thanks for the update. We'll take her off our list."

I told the group what I had learned, and Auntie's threat list now had two crossed-out names and no other suspects. The list of people who had something to lose if the marriage came to light was growing.

"In terms of Ken's family," Gertie said, "that only leaves Daisy. Hard to imagine, but let's not leave anyone out."

Mary chimed in. "My, but she was certainly outspoken about how the appearance of Mark might disrupt her life and her money. They were the first things to come to her mind."

The Professor sighed. "The marriage is now out in the open. What's left to be discovered is who killed Summer and Auntie. I suspect the person who threatened Kelly today is the murderer."

We all looked at Rudy's list. That left Ken's family.

Ken's kingdom threatened.

Sue Ellen's marriage problem revealed, her children's inheritance in question, and a possible financial impact.

Anthony could lose his lifestyle. He implied he wanted a change, but was that the truth? And did drugs play a role?

Edie's business dream. Might it go bust?

John's business plans disrupted.

Daisy and money concerns, angered about being intruded upon.

Had one of them signed for the packet that provided proof of Ken's marriage to Diane? If so, which one? Had they killed to keep it from being revealed?

All the people on this list had reasons to keep the marriage from coming to light. The murderer was possibly among them. And they didn't want to be discovered. The list was of my potential attackers.

And they'd all been at the gardens today.

Chapter 21

"The only list we have with names and motives is the one connected with the marriage," the Professor said as he stared at the chart. "It's possible Mary's attack is still connected to Auntie in some way, or it could have been random. However, I think we should move forward with the assumption that there was a case of mistaken identity and Martha was the intended target."

Rudy nodded. "With the three of them gone, no one would know about Ken and Diane."

I shifted in my chair and arched my back, loosening tight muscles. "The marriage is out in the open. The murderer's plan didn't work, and now the killer fears getting caught. I believe that's what provoked the attack on me."

"Martha, if indeed you are the person the assailant was after," the Professor said, "that means you need to be careful."

Martha frowned. "But people know about the marriage now."

"Yes, but you're the only person living who witnessed it," the Professor replied. "I know you filed the paperwork, but the killer might feel there's still a way to keep the marriage from being considered valid if there's no one to verify it. It's a stretch, but I think it's best to not take a chance."

Martha's frown stayed in place. "I'm used to being very independent, and a lot of people rely on me, so I can't really just stay inside."

Mary reached for her sister's hand. "For a while, until we get this straightened out, please don't go anywhere alone."

"Ivan and I can take turns going places with you," Rudy said. "And we'd be happy to help with your projects."

Ivan nodded in agreement.

"That's nice of you two." Martha sighed. "Okay. I'll give it a try."

The Professor spun his pencil. "It'll be hard for us to figure out where the people on the list were on Wednesday afternoon. I can ask Auntie's closest neighbors if they noticed anything, but her house is out of sight of anyone."

"I think we should concentrate on Kelly's attack," Gertie said. "All of the people were at the gardens today. Maybe we can eliminate some of them, if nothing else. I'll talk to members of the class and ask them what they saw this afternoon. The instructor assigned us to search for examples of a variety of plants. We all went in separate directions."

Martha rubbed Sergeant under his chin. "I'll talk to the folks who were helping set up the parking lot. Maybe we can piece together an alibi for Anthony and his friend. Tank's name isn't up there, but he was with Anthony during what might have been a drug deal. It wouldn't hurt to know where he was."

"Muscle man and pink lady on sticks ate lunch at the Brown Bear Deli around eleven-thirty," Ivan volunteered.

"Good to know," I said. "But Daisy was still at the gardens when I was attacked."

Princess gave a yip, announcing it was time for Mary to pay attention to her.

Mary picked up the Chihuahua and cuddled her. "I've known the manager of the gardens for years. I'll see what he knows. With the police there, he won't be surprised by my questions. I'm sure the officers will have already asked him to check with his staff."

"Anything else anyone can think of?" asked the Professor.

The negative head shaking said it was time to adjourn.

Martha and Mary packed up their charges and left with the Professor and Gertie. The others went their separate ways.

I went to my room, brushed my hair, and collected my purse. A visit with Scott would be a nice change from discussing motives for murder. I peeked in the parlor. Phil and Andy had arrived. They were unpacking at the large table, where we served appetizers.

Andy bore the title cheese monger and supplied my inn and Ridley House with artisanal cheeses. When I first met him and sampled his products, my taste buds quickly informed me this wasn't the brick cheese I bought at chain grocery stores. The calories of his favorite food, cheese, gave him an ongoing battle with his waistline.

"Hi," I said and entered the room.

Andy hurried over and gave me a hug. "Kelly, so good to see you. We just arrived. I brought your favorite cheese."

My mouth watered as I thought of the layers of firm, tangy Double Gloucester combined with creamy, blue-veined Stilton cheese to create a divine combination that was beautiful to look at and wonderful to taste. "The Huntsman?"

"That's it." He dove into a small ice chest and pulled out said cheese and began to unwrap it.

"I'll have to pass for now, Andy. I have an appointment."

"It'll be waiting for you," he said with a smile.

Phil finished placing two wine bottles on the table, along with glasses. His gray curls glistened in the light. "Did you get your dancing shoes out?"

"No, but I will. Helen gave me your message."

"I'll be line dancing at two-thirty in Sunflower Park."

I walked over and looked at the labels on the bottles he'd put out. The stately greyhound with the flowing red scarf and tucked wing on his side proclaimed it to be from the Flying Dog Winery. Phil had used it when I had my first wine-tasting lesson. Next to it was a bottle of sauvignon blanc.

"This is a new wine just released by the same winery." Phil pointed to the white wine. "I'll put some in the refrigerator, and you can try it later."

The label had the same slender breed of dog, only this one was white and had a jeweled necklace around her throat. From under long lashes, she appeared to be looking coyly at the other dog. Her wing was slightly raised.

"Thanks. I'll look forward to giving it a try."

Andy and Phil supplied a number of inns and restaurants and had been coming to the area for a long time. I wondered if they might know something that would help our investigation.

"Have either of you met a fortune teller called Auntie or a woman named Amy Winter who assisted her and went by the name Summer?"

Phil stretched to his tallest height, a little shorter than me, which made him about five foot five, and raised his eyebrows. "I, Philopoimen Xanthis, Greek and raised in the old country, knew Despina Manyotis, also raised in the old country, quite well. There are very strong cultural ties in the Greek community."

Andy finished arranging his cheese platter. "She was a nice lady."

"You knew her as well?" I asked him.

"No, not really. Phil took me to visit her once when I was having stomach issues. She gave me an herbal remedy that worked like a charm. No more discomfort."

Phil poured a couple of glasses of wine. "I was sad to hear of her passing."

"How did you learn about it?"

"I know her sisters as well. They got in touch with me. Why do you ask about her and the other woman, Summer? I met her assistant briefly a couple of times."

"The Silver Sentinels don't feel their deaths were accidental."

"Ahh... Auntie and Summer's poisoning." He picked up the glass of wine he had poured and examined it, holding it up to the light. "I agree with them."

"What makes you think it wasn't an accident?"

"Auntie's been harvesting herbs for years. She knew what she was doing."

"That's what the Sentinels believe as well."

"Her sisters invited me to her service on Sunday and the next one in forty days."

"Why are there two?"

"Greeks believe the soul stays present for that length of time."

I remembered the sisters saying Auntie would be present for a while.

"I wish you all luck in finding out who did it." Phil swirled the wine, sniffed it, and took a sip. "She was a kind person, wanting to help others and teach them how to care for themselves using Mother Nature's resources. Her sisters are the same. They'll continue Auntie's good work here. Adrasteia will inherit the Book of Secrets, as she is the eldest. They have a family obligation to continue the tradition."

"You know about the book?"

"Auntie showed it to me once. We went through the genealogy lines together. We were curious to see if our families were ever connected."

"Were they?"

"No, but both of us recognized a number of names our parents had mentioned."

"Did you know the book is missing?"

Phil stopped what he was doing and put his glass on the table. "What do you mean?"

I told him what Mary and I had discovered.

"Adrasteia and Fotini are caring women, but I sure wouldn't want to be in the shoes of the person who stole that book. If you believe in spirits, telling the future, perhaps curses and magic, the sisters are very powerful. That book is centuries old. Many believe it has a life of its own, a special energy."

"They mentioned that Despina's spirit might help locate it."

"Wouldn't doubt it," he said. "They'll get the book back."

Andy had left with his cooler and now returned with a tray. He placed the wine and cheese on it.

"The Huntsman has your name on it," he said.

They left to do their sampling, and I went to the workroom to touch base with Helen.

She was in the process of taking off her apron. A bowl of flour on the counter sat next to an open container of sugar and several baskets of blueberries. I noticed two clean towels on the divider.

"What are those for?" I asked.

"The Nelsens asked for a couple more."

"I'm on my way out. I can take them."

"Thanks, Kelly. I was about to start baking for tomorrow's breakfast."

I picked up the towels and headed for the Maritime Suite. Anthony, on the landing above, walked from his room and entered the open door of the family area. I jogged up the steps, anxious to make my delivery and leave.

I walked to the open door and stopped.

Ken's clenched fist waved in front of Anthony's face. "I don't ever want you to bring any of your druggie friends around our family again. That big guy Daisy was with, I've seen him on our property. Not ever again, do you understand?"

Anthony's smooth face reflected no emotion. He didn't move, just continued to stare at his father.

Sue Ellen caught my eye on the other side of the two and shrugged her shoulders and spread her hands apologetically.

Ken rounded on Daisy, who was a few feet away from him.

"And you, I don't want you seeing that man again. I'm forbidding it."

I taught school for a while and had seen the look that Daisy gave her father. It shouted she'd be seeing Tank again, and I guessed she'd do it as soon as possible.

Chapter 22

Sue Ellen skirted around behind Ken and took the towels from me. She mouthed, "Sorry."

I nodded and hurried down the stairs and over to my Jeep, ready for a change of scene. Looking at my watch, I saw I'd be a couple of minutes late meeting Scott.

I hadn't been to Corrigan's place before, but the directions were straightforward. The area I drove through had redwood trees growing in abundance, interspersed with inviting green meadows occasionally dotted with a pond. The temperature rose with every mile inland. In less than ten minutes, I saw the turnoff.

Pink and white oleanders, the hardy go-to plant of Californians, lined the paved drive. The bushes grew abundantly on the sides of freeways and provided privacy barriers for many homes. A single-story, wide, rambling structure with a covered porch the length of the front of the building appeared. It reminded me of Wyoming ranch houses. Side rooms gave it a U-shape and the feeling of welcoming, open arms.

Scott was leaning on a porch post, waiting for me.

I parked the Jeep and got out. "Hi! Sorry I'm late. I needed to deliver towels to one of the guests, and there was a bit of a delay."

"No problem," he said. "Guests always come first, as we know. Come on in."

He opened the screen door, held it for me, and gestured for me to enter. An exceptionally large living room full of comfortable-looking couches and overstuffed chairs greeted me. Soft throw blankets of different shades adorned the backs of the furniture. A stone fireplace dominated one end. Tables full of magazines and books were within easy reach of anyone wanting to read. The room made me want to curl up and dig into a good book.

"We can stop right here as far as I'm concerned," I said.

"I know what you mean. Michael wants people to relax and take on a different mind-set when they come here as a retreat, getting away from the craziness that business sometimes produces. He succeeded really well, I'd say."

"I totally agree."

"Let's go to the kitchen. There's a nice area to sit in, and I made some sun tea."

He led the way into a commercial-size kitchen that housed an abundance of stainless-steel appliances. The spacious room could accommodate a number of people working at the same time. Scott pointed to a table with a couple of chairs next to a turquoise window seat at the end of the room. A vase filled with long sprigs of yellow gladiolus sat in the center of it.

I chose the window seat. The view showed a grassy meadow with . . . llamas? Was I seeing things?

"Tell me I'm not hallucinating and there are Peruvian beasts of burden out there."

Scott laughed. "They provide wool for weaving. They arrived yesterday and are part of Michael's plans for the center."

I looked out again. A small brown-and-white animal had raised its head and seemed to be staring at me. Large brown eyes, a long nose, and triangular ears topped a long, graceful, furry neck.

"City boy to llama wrangler. You made a big leap," I told Scott.

Scott walked to the refrigerator, opened it, and took out a pitcher. "Hold on. Big city to little village was enough of a change. The man who tends the produce garden is in charge of the llamas. A word of warning. They spit if they get mad at you."

"I know. I hope you haven't found out the hard way."

"No. I was warned. I smile at them, wave, and keep my distance. I don't know what makes a llama upset, and I'm not taking any chances."

"My parents don't have any on the ranch, but we've talked about adding them. They're good pack animals, which we could use for our overnight camping trips. They supply wool, as you said, and make fun pets. We thought our summer guests might enjoy them."

Scott put a tall glass filled with ice and an orange slice in front of me. "I haven't had time to get together what I need for my cooking, but brewing herbal sun tea seemed like an easy start to my stay here." He poured me some.

"My mom does that, too. She says it has a smoother taste."

"I agree with her. There's no harshness, and it doesn't cloud up, which sometimes happens."

I took a sip. It wasn't overly strong, and the orange gave it a hint of citrus. I found the chilled beverage refreshing in the warmer inland area. "Tasty. What kind is it?"

"I use green tea, which is healthy for you, but I sometimes find it a bit bitter, so I combine it with mint tea to mask that flavor. The orange slice adds a bit of sweetness and a wonderful scent."

I had learned about Scott's cooking interest on his last visit. I'd never been around a man who enjoyed stepping into a kitchen. What a delightful new experience!

He poured a glass for himself and put the pitcher in the refrigerator. His face lost its brightness as he sat on the window seat. "You said you'd tell me what happened at the gardens today. I'd like to hear it."

The deaths of Auntie and Summer had caused the attack on me. I needed to share it all.

"There's a lot to it, so it's best you get comfortable."

He settled into the corner, leaning on a throw pillow. "Begin. I'm ready."

It took a while, as I had forewarned him.

When I was done, he shook his head. "How is it such a nice-looking group of elderly people manages to get you into one scrape after another?"

I looked at him. "They don't make me get involved. I want to help find the truth, and that's their goal as well."

"I decided to take this job to find out what living in an area like this would be like. I know you love it, and I've never experienced it. I'd hoped we'd have some time to see what . . . a normal life would be like here in Redwood Cove."

Oh my gosh, had he come here because of me? Conflicting emotions raced through me. It felt like excitement was winning over fear.

"Normal doesn't seem to be part of the equation with the Silver Sentinels," Scott said, "because that word doesn't pair with murder."

"They're only trying to do what's right."

"I know. There's a phrase that says if you can't beat them, join them. It's not quite a fit here, but there are some similarities." He leaned back into the cushions. "I've only met them in passing and would like to know them better. I don't have anything special I can whip together for food right now, but how about seeing if they can make it for bacon and eggs tomorrow morning around nine?"

Scott and the Sentinels. I knew they'd love it. But was I ready for Scott to enter this part of my life?

I hesitated, then decided it couldn't hurt to give it a try. "Well . . . okay."

The Professor was at the top of the Sentinel's phone list, so I selected his number. I told him about Scott's invitation, and he said he'd contact the others and get back to me.

"The Professor will call me back."

"Great. If there's any way I can help bring this situation to an end, I'd like to do it. Incidentally, I talked to one of the suspects on your list."

"Which one?"

"Anthony. But it was after the attack on you, so it doesn't give him an alibi. However, the man who runs the homeless shelter was in charge of organizing the parking area today. He's supposed to call me this afternoon. I'll see what I can find out from him."

I nodded and took a sip of tea. "I know Michael's overall goals for this place. I think it's wonderful that he wants to help the community. I thought about it today. The things that make Redwood Cove unique also bring problems and challenges."

"It's an interesting project. Let's go for a walk, and I'll show you some of what we have planned and introduce you to Jim Patterson, who works here."

We went out a back door and down a sidewalk, headed toward the llamas. There was a walkway to the left, and Scott followed it. We rounded a corner, and a large garden area, much of it in raised boxes, came into view. A man with a wide-brimmed straw hat was bent over, weeding.

"Jim," Scott said, "I'd like you to meet Kelly Jackson, manager at Redwood Cove Bed-and-Breakfast."

The man rose, slowly unbending his tall frame, and walked over to us. "Glad to meet you."

The hand he extended was wide and flat, the nails short, with only a small crust of dirt showing. The earthy scent of freshly tilled soil filled the air. Jim's face had a serene look like the one my mom had when she tended her plants. She'd told me it made her feel connected to the natural world around her.

"Jim manages the garden and is caring for the llamas as well. He'll be leading classes on how to grow your own vegetables at home and will supervise the area where people can have a plot to plant what they want. One of our goals is to create healthier, happier lives for people, and fresh food contributes to that."

"Nice to meet you, Jim. I was raised on a Wyoming ranch, and we grew as much of our own food as possible."

"Maybe we can compare notes sometime," Jim said.

"Sure. I'd like that. Mom and Dad are always open to new ideas."

Scott tilted his head toward the path. We said good-bye and continued on.

"Another thing Michael wants to do is provide a haven for military personnel returning from combat who are having trouble adjusting."

As he shared this, we entered a grove of exceptionally tall, majestic redwood trees. Sunbeams slanting through their branches and needlelike leaves created nature's stained glass and made for an almost cathedral type of feeling. The golden shafts cut through the darkness. Small cottages dotted the path ahead.

"This area will be for veterans. There's a family section, as well as accommodations for singles."

A man with a large dog by his side was coming down the path toward us.

"Here's someone else I'd like you to meet, Peter Wilson."

The dog looked like a Bernese mountain dog, with black curly hair and tricolored facial markings of white, brown, and black.

"Peter, this is Kelly Jackson. She works for Resorts International and manages the Redwood Cove B and B."

"Nice to meet you." He extended his hand.

We shook. "Beautiful dog," I said. "Can I pet it?"

"Absolutely. Jake loves attention."

I knelt in front of the canine, and he leaned into me. His warmth seeped into my body. He pushed his head against mine. My shoulders relaxed and dropped a few notches. I hadn't realized how much tension I was carrying. The release almost brought tears to my eyes.

Scott stroked the dog's head. "Peter trains dogs for veterans suffering from PTSD."

Scott's phone beeped, and he excused himself and walked a few feet away.

Peter nodded. "Were you by any chance feeling tense just now?"

"I was, though I didn't realize how much until I felt it release."

"What he just did was provide deep pressure for a calming effect. When someone is having a panic attack, he'll push against their chest or abdomen, depending on where they are and what position they're in."

"What other techniques are the dogs taught?" I asked.

"There's a long list. We match our training to the needs of the future owner. For example, crowd control is another area where Jake knows what to do. He'll repeatedly circle his owner to keep people at a distance. It's important for some veterans that they don't get startled by having someone bump into them."

"Jake went for his final exam today," Scott said as he joined us and looked at the trainer. "How did he do?"

"Passed with flying colors. He's ready to go to his new home."

"Michael wants to start a training program here," Scott said to me. "The dogs all come from shelters. It's a win-win situation for all parties."

Peter said good-bye and left with Jake. What a gift my incredible boss, Michael Corrigan, was providing. I hoped others would follow his role model.

My cell phone rang, and I answered it.

"Hello, my dear. Tomorrow's a go," the Professor said. "I'll bring freshly squeezed orange juice."

"I'm sure Scott doesn't expect people to bring anything."

"My dear, it's part of who we are. Mary will bring a fruit crisp, Gertie wheat bread, and Rudy and Ivan will have smoked salmon, cream cheese, and bagels."

"Okay. That sounds great. I know better than to argue. I'll let him know."

"The Sentinels can make it tomorrow," I said to Scott and shared with him what they'd be bringing.

He laughed. "It doesn't sound like I'll be providing much of the breakfast, but I'm glad it will work out."

The breakfast party was on. Scott was ready to get to know the Silver Sentinels. And it seemed I was ready to let that happen.

"The phone call was from the manager of the homeless shelter. I didn't have to question him about Anthony. When I asked him how the day went, he said fine after he shooed away the blonde in tight pants hanging around Tank and Anthony. His guys weren't getting any work done while she was there. That was during the time you were attacked."

Daisy, Tank, and Anthony had an alibi for the assault on me. That didn't clear them of the murders, but every piece of the jigsaw puzzle we could put in place was a step closer to an answer.

Chapter 23

The path curved its way through the trees, finding natural openings for it to continue on its way. The only sound was the occasional twitter or call of a bird. Up close I could see the cottages were small log cabins.

Scott went up to one of the cottages. "Let me show you inside," he said as he opened the door.

Multicolored braided oval rugs covered the hardwood floor. The walls on the inside were made from pale yellow, smooth-textured logs. Neatly stacked firewood sat next to a wood-burning stove.

The living room area had a couch and a chair similar to the ones in the main house—the type that invited you to settle in with one of the soft throws covering the backs of the furniture. Off to the right was a small kitchen area and a dining table next to a window.

"Over here is the bedroom." He opened a door revealing a queen-size bed covered with a golden-hued down comforter.

An open door in the room showed part of a white-tiled counter and sink.

Large windows dominated the rooms, allowing filtered sunlight through the redwood trees to enter and frame the lush glen outside. Dappled sunlight decorated the room with nature's touch.

A small, black flat box with a large white button on it sat in one corner of the living room floor.

"What is that?"

"That's another skill Jake's been taught. That's a K-nine Rescue Alarm phone."

I went over and knelt down next to it. "How does it work?"

"The dog is taught to press the button with its paw in certain situations. The phone is programmed with the number of the person who should be called if there's a crisis. Depending on the person's history and what he or she needs, it could be nine-one-one or a relative, for example. That's why much of the training is geared to an individual."

"What dogs contribute to our lives never ceases to amaze me," I said.

"I agree. Let's head back."

As Scott closed the door, I surveyed the bucolic setting. It was easy to imagine it being a healing place for people.

As we walked, Scott said, "We've contacted a number of local businesses to line up jobs and potential opportunities for the veterans to learn new skills. There are restaurants, inns, and a woodworking school that are interested in helping so far."

"It's nice to hear the community is pitching in."

He nodded and pointed to an area off to our right. "Jim wants to plant a meditation garden near here, creating a place to promote a sense of peace, calmness, and serenity. He's been doing a lot of research. It'll have a water element, arrangements of stones, something fragrant, like maybe lavender, and, of course, lots of plants."

"Sounds like a good idea."

After a day that had revolved around murder, talk of positive plans acted like a tonic, and I felt a surge of energy.

We passed the llamas grazing on the heretofore untouched pasture, quite content to be the first creature guests to enjoy the grassy meal. The brown-and-white one eyed us. It seemed more interactive than the others. I started toward it.

"Uhh . . . Kelly, let's keep moving. I want to show you the list of ideas we have for the community center." Scott eyed the llama suspiciously.

The llama was chewing with a rotating movement and didn't lose eye contact with Scott.

He was out of his element, but I gave him credit. I loved that he was giving it a try. I imagined myself in New York City. I'd probably be eyeing the taxis, crazy traffic, and crowded sidewalks the same way.

We entered the kitchen of the main house and sat at the table. Scott talked about what was being considered. I'd already read most of it in company memos.

"My table at the event tomorrow will have these things listed on a board and flyers inviting people to come to a meeting. I'm also forming a community planning committee."

"I hope Michael plans on encouraging others to adopt a give-back model like this."

"He does. Once everything's in place, he's going to have a special week where he'll invite some of the movers and shakers he knows to see what he's created. And he knows a lot of those people."

I checked my watch. "I'd better get going. Thanks for the tour."

"You're welcome." Scott put his hand on my shoulder. "Kelly, please be careful. You've got someone very scared."

"I know. I'm going straight back to the inn and won't venture out anywhere tonight."

"I look forward to meeting with the Sentinels tomorrow. As I said before, I want to help in any way I can to get the problem you're dealing with resolved and see what a normal life in an area like this is about." He gave me a skeptical look. "Though I'm beginning to wonder if that exists."

He walked me to my vehicle.

I got in, put down the window, and said with a grin, "What should I bring tomorrow for the potluck?"

He laughed. "Don't you dare bring anything. You know I've planned on doing it all. It's something I enjoy. Plus the Silver Sentinels are bringing a lot."

"Okay." I understood where he was coming from. Still, if everyone else was bringing something . . .

The ride back to Redwood Cove Bed-and-Breakfast was short. I pulled into the driveway and parked. John and Edie's car was next to mine, and they were both standing in the parking lot. She held a huge bouquet of flowers. He was dressed in a suit and tie. He bent down, gave her a hug, then got in their car and drove off. Edie stood looking after him, a smile on her face.

I got out and went to her. "Beautiful flowers. Do you need a vase?"

"I do, actually. John feels so bad. He promised he wouldn't work this weekend, but one of the managers is ill, and he needs to take his place. We were going to go to dinner with Ken and Sue Ellen. He knows he didn't have to do this." She held up the flowers. "I understand he needs to go. But it's his way of saying he's sorry."

"If you'd like, I can cut off the ends and put them in a vase with food and water."

"Thanks, Kelly. That's really sweet of you. I appreciate it." She handed the bouquet to me.

"I'll come to your room with the flowers shortly."

Edie walked toward the building housing their rooms. Her long, flowered dress billowed around her legs in the breeze. She clutched the mint green sweater that matched the pattern on her skirt around her shoulders. Wisps of her blond hair danced around her face.

Inside, I put the flowers on the counter and retrieved an appropriate-sized vase and put water in it. I trimmed the stems, found plant food, and mixed it with water. Peach-colored roses, white lilies, and deep blue delphinium created a delightful bouquet. I spent a couple of minutes arranging them. I'd let Edie do the fine tuning.

My ankle throbbed, and my hands hurt from my recent near-death experience, but I pushed through it like I'd do if I was on the ranch. Aches and pains were inevitable when you worked with livestock, like an ornery sow protecting her piglets or a horse that didn't want to be ridden. Then there was the occasional escaped chicken that didn't want to get caught, beaks and sharp nails letting you know how unhappy it was. Throw in fixing fences and a few splinters got added to the mix.

I sighed out loud just as Helen came in.

"You sound really tired, Kelly."

"It's been a long day, physically and mentally. I'm looking forward to a quiet evening."

"I'm fixing a meatloaf tonight. Nothing fancy. You're welcome to some."

"That's our favorite family comfort food. Mom fixes it whenever it's been a particularly trying day. And it's the first meal we have when a blizzard starts and we're spending time outside in the freezing cold. I won't say I wanted the snowstorms to happen, but we all knew it was meatloaf day when it really began to come down."

"Then I take it that's a yes."

"Yes, and thank you." I looked in the refrigerator and saw the Huntsman. Perfect. Artisanal cheese and homemade meatloaf!

I headed to the Maritime Suite with the flowers. As I started up the stairs, a door slammed. Daisy appeared at the top. She frowned and moved back when she saw me. Could her jeans be tighter and her heels higher than earlier? I didn't think it was possible, but they looked that way.

"Good evening, Daisy," I said.

She smacked her gum. "Hi." She slipped around me. Daisy went down the stairs as quickly as the unsteady heels allowed.

I had to admit I didn't miss my teaching days and students like her. There'd been a lot of sweet kids, but there'd been Daisys, too. I wondered if seeing Tank was part of her evening's plans.

I knocked on Edie's door.

She opened it. "Kelly, those look wonderful. Come on in."

I was happy with the way the room had turned out. The bed-spread's blue sailing ships on a background of white gave an upbeat feel to the room. The lush, royal blue carpet was in the same color family as the light blue couch resting on it.

"Where do you want them?"

"I wasn't expecting John to give me the flowers." Edie looked around. "Here, let's put them on the coffee table."

She'd put her sweater over a pile of what looked like books and magazines on the table. "I'll put these on the bed for now," she said as she reached for them.

Edie grabbed them up in her arms and went to toss the stack onto the bed. The load must have been heavy, because she struggled to hold onto them. The pile fell apart as she went to throw it on the bed-spread and landed on the floor, scattering printed matter across the floor.

"Here, I'll help." I put the flowers down and picked up a copy of *Good Housekeeping*. Next to it was a *Sunset*.

"No, it's okay. I can do it," Edie said, reaching for the remaining pile as I picked up another magazine.

It had been on top of a book with a metal cover made of copper inlaid with jewels of different colors. Delicate engraving covered its surface. The book gleamed in the light. I knew what it was, but the photographs I'd seen hadn't done it justice. If the stones were dia-monds, rubies, and emeralds, which is what they looked like, the book was worth a fortune. I recognized the Greek lettering on the cover. It was the Book of Secrets.

Chapter 24

I froze. Then looked at Edie. She picked up Auntie's book, put it on the bed, and covered it with her sweater.

Did Edie kill Auntie and Summer to get the Book of Secrets for her business?

"Thanks again for your help with the flowers." She headed for the door, opened it, and looked at me. "I'd better get ready for dinner."

I didn't move. "Edie, I know what that book is."

Edie tilted her head. "What do you mean? Which one are you talking about? There are several in the pile."

"The Book of Secrets. Despina's sisters want it back."

"Oh, that one." Edie's face drained of color. She looked at her sweater concealing the book. "I wanted to be sure I had everything written down correctly, and Auntie said there were a few more formulas she wanted me to have. After I checked my notes and found the additional remedies, I was going to return it."

"It's been reported stolen."

"Heavens, I didn't *steal* it. I planned on giving it back."

"You need to call the police."

"Of course. I'll be happy to let them know I have it." She still stood at the open door, a clear indication she wanted me to leave.

I was determined that Despina's sisters were going to get their family heirloom back. "No time like the present. I've got my phone right here, and Deputy Sheriff Stanton's number is on it." I selected it and punched the number before she could say anything.

"Kelly, I'll—"

"Hello, Deputy Stanton, I have a guest here who has something she wants you to know."

I handed Edie the phone. Her lips were clamped tightly together, and she paused for a second before taking it.

"Hello. My name is Edie Brockton," she said, and her eyes narrowed. "I . . . borrowed something from Despina Manyotis's house. I just found out you are looking for it. I have her book of remedies."

Borrowed and planned on giving it back? Or took it and planned on keeping it? She was good with words. Auntie would never have let her take it, so she must've been dead when Edie took it. She'd been careful not to indicate that Auntie had given it to her.

"Certainly. I'd be happy to talk to you." She listened for another minute, then handed me back the phone. "He'll be here in about ten minutes." She stared at me. "You didn't need to do that, Kelly."

"I know her sisters are anxious to get the book back. They're dealing with Despina's death, so the less they have to worry about, the better."

Edie nodded. "You're right." She sat on the bed and uncovered the book. "Despina didn't tell her sisters about our partnership. She didn't think they'd be in favor of me learning so many of the formulas. Auntie cared about helping people and felt she could do much more in partnership with me."

"Was she going to work in the store? If so, she would have had a hard time hiding her connection with you."

"No, she wasn't. We'd both put the remedies together, but she'd do the more unusual ones. I wanted a last look at the book because I didn't think the sisters would let me see it."

Would they share a family treasure called the Book of Secrets? I didn't think so, nor did I think they wanted someone outside of the family reading what was in there.

"Kelly, can I meet the deputy in one of the rooms in the inn? The last thing I want is for Ken to see him coming into my room and then barging in here wanting to know what's going on."

I certainly agreed with her there. "That's a good idea. I can find someplace for the two of you."

She put on her sweater and picked up the book. Nothing had been listed for the conference room after the meeting with the Silver Sentinels. If Helen had added something, then they could meet in the office. I texted Stanton to tell him where he could find us.

Rather than walk through the inn with Edie carrying something that looked like it came from *The Arabian Nights*, I planned on using the private entrance.

"Let's go in the side door. We can avoid any questions about the book."

For the second time that day, I entered the building wanting to not be seen. I ushered Edie into the empty conference room and closed the door. I checked the posted schedule and saw it was clear for the rest of the day. Edie put the book on the table.

The seconds ticked by in an awkward silence. I decided I had nothing to lose by asking her some questions. She could always refuse to answer.

"When did you get the book?"

"Friday morning. I heard about the accidental deaths. Auntie had said there were a few more formulas she wanted me to have, and I wanted to get the additional remedies."

"How did you get in? The house was locked."

"I knew where Auntie hid her spare key. She wanted me to have access in case I needed some of the herbs."

"Mary said Auntie was very secretive about where the book was kept and very few people knew where it was."

Edie caressed the metal cover. "She was. I went to see her one day. The door was open, and I called out her name. She didn't answer, so I went to find her. I found her in the pantry with her back to me. I saw her take out the book. She didn't know I was there. I went back to the kitchen to wait for her."

It all sounded plausible. They might not be able to charge her with anything. No forced entry, gathering information for their business venture, not yet a crime scene. A knock at the door proved to be Deputy Sheriff Stanton. I excused myself and went to the kitchen so they could have some privacy.

We were into appetizer and wine time. Helen came in with a stack of empty plates and put them in the sink.

"Do you need any help?"

"No, it's quiet. A lot of people are still out enjoying the day." She glanced out the window to where the squad car was parked. "Is that Bill?"

"Yes. One of our guests had . . . something belonging to Auntie she needed to return. Her sisters thought it had been stolen, so there was a police report."

I wasn't convinced Edie had planned to return it, but with the business connection, it was going to be hard to prove she had stolen it.

"I put a dinner plate for you in the refrigerator."

I opened it and saw a very generous helping of meatloaf, cooked zucchini, and multicolored rice.

"Thank you so much." Yes, life here really worked for me.

I went into the parlor and saw one couple sitting in front of the fire. Not wanting to disturb them, I went back into the kitchen to wait for Stanton to finish talking with Edie and began preparing a food order.

I was about halfway through the list when Stanton came in. He carried the shiny, copper-covered book cradled in one arm.

Helen asked him, "Would you like some coffee?"

"You bet." He put the Book of Secrets on the counter.

I remembered what Phil had said about the book having a power, a life of its own. That was easy to imagine as the book seemed to shimmer in the bright overhead lights. Engravings covered the entire top and side, except for where precious stones had been embedded. A title in what looked like Greek writing was centered on the cover. Gold and silver inlay added to its luster.

I reached for it and was surprised at its warmth. It felt like it was alive. I'd expected the metal to be cold.

I pulled my hand back.

Wait. Stanton had been carrying it, so it was simply his body that had warmed it. Of course, that was it. I picked it up, turned it over, and saw that the back matched the front, except for the title.

"It's a real treasure just as a work of art. I can't imagine what its value is," I said. "And that's without factoring in the worth of the information it contains."

"I agree. I've called the sisters, and they're on the way. The sooner it's back in their hands, the better. They're at Auntie's, so they'll be here soon."

Helen put a cup of coffee in front of him.

"Edie chose to leave the way you both came in. Didn't want to talk to anyone."

"Is she going to be charged with anything?"

"Not unless Adrasteia and Fotini want to press charges. Edie had an explanation for everything."

I agreed with him. At least Despina's family would have their property back.

The door burst open, and Tommy and Fred rushed in, Allie right behind them. Tommy skidded to a stop, his eyes on the book where it sat next to Stanton. His mouth dropped, as did Allie's. Daniel accompanied them in, and I thought his mouth might do the same.

"Wow!" Tommy closed his mouth, then opened it again. "Wow!"

Allie whispered, "It's like something from a fairy tale."

Indeed it was.

"Can we touch it?" she asked.

"I don't see why not. Wash and dry your hands first," Stanton said.

The doorbell rang, and Helen went to answer it.

The kids did as instructed, then Allie lightly ran her hand over the cover. Tommy followed her lead. Just as he started to trace the Greek letters with his finger, Adrasteia and Fotini entered the kitchen. Their robes seemed to have a life of their own as they swirled around the fast-moving, tall women. Medusa-like strands of gray hair, escapees from their black scarves, waved around.

"The Book!" Adrasteia exclaimed.

Tommy's hand seemed attached to the cover. He hadn't moved since they'd entered the room. His eyes grew large. Fred put himself between Tommy and the sisters.

"I . . . I . . . I . . ." Tommy stuttered. He snatched his hand away from the book.

Fotini smiled at Tommy. "No need to worry, little *pedthe*." She picked up the Book of Secrets and held it close to her chest and looked upward. "Thank you, Despina. I knew you would help bring it home."

Adrasteia addressed Stanton. "This woman who had it said she borrowed it." She shook her head. "Auntie would never have let someone take the book."

Deputy Sheriff Stanton said, "She went to Despina's place after she died. She was going into business with Auntie, opening a store, and wanted some of the formulas she'd been promised. She'd been told where the house key was kept, so she'd been given permission to enter the home."

"Business? Auntie stayed home. And this woman knew where the book was kept?"

"That's all I know. I questioned her, and she assured me she planned on contacting you and returning the book."

I didn't know how much backstory Edie had given Stanton. I explained how she knew where the book was hidden. There was a gray area there. She hadn't been given access to the book, just promised some of what was in it.

"Auntie wasn't going to work in the store, just provide remedies," I said.

The sisters mumbled something to each other in Greek.

Adrasteia threw back her head. "We have the book. That is what matters."

Fotini looked at me. "You were the messenger between Despina and the Book of Secrets. Despina would want you at her memorial service. You and the other woman who worked with Auntie are invited to attend. It will be held at Auntie's house on Sunday at eleven. People bring food. We eat, we drink, we talk, we think of Auntie."

"Thank you. I'll let Mary know."

In a flurry of moving black robes, they swept out as they'd come in, book in hand.

Had Despina helped locate the book? If so, would she help find her killer?

Chapter 25

The next morning, I was pleased to find that my hands and ankle had improved. It was probably the great meatloaf dinner I'd eaten last night. Not quite one of Auntie's homeopathic remedies, but medicinal in its own way. It had certainly made me feel a lot better.

I thought about the day ahead. Scott and the Silver Sentinels. This should be a fun as well as an interesting morning. I looked forward to seeing them interact with each other. I took a little extra time with my makeup since I'd be representing the inns of the area today. My sister would be proud. She'd tried so often to get me to work on my appearance more. Growing up, the horses didn't mind that I didn't use eyeliner, and they were all I cared about. I had yielded when I met my ex, then gave it up when he left.

Makeup done, I joined Helen in the workroom. The breakfast baskets were ready, and we each did our deliveries. I thanked my lucky stars, or maybe it was Despina, that Ken didn't appear as I dropped off the muffins, coffee, and fruit. John's car was parked in the lot, so he'd made it back at some point. I wondered if he knew the story of the book.

For my offering for the potluck breakfast, as it was turning out to be, I'd decided on a cheese platter. Cheese for breakfast was common in Europe, and we had such a nice selection, thanks to Andy, I thought it would be fun to take some. Gertie was bringing bread, so I put some crackers in, along with the plate. There would be way more food than we'd all eat, but that was what made events like this fun—plenty of food and a wide variety. I made a second platter for Despina's memorial service.

I placed everything in a sturdy bag and put it behind the driver's seat. The fog had burned off early, and it was clear blue skies all the way to Corrigan's place. I parked and saw the little brown-and-white llama looking at me. The pasture they were in came all the way to the front of the house. Taking out the food, I went over to the animal and scratched its shoulder.

When we'd considered getting llamas for the ranch, I'd done some research. They were considered very friendly, social animals for the most part. However, Scott was right about the fact that they could and would, in some instances, spit. They could regurgitate their entire stomach contents and spit it up to ten feet away. Usually that happened when they felt threatened, but sometimes it could be just because they were in a bad mood.

This little guy seemed like a happy camper as he chewed and wiggled his ears. His huge brown eyes assured me he had no negative intentions toward me. I took a few minutes and shared with him some of what had been happening. He nodded his head up and down as if in agreement. In reality, he was probably getting rid of an annoying fly. I walked along the fence toward the front door, and he followed beside me like a dog.

Scott answered my knock, wearing a full-length white apron, dishtowel tucked into the tied strings in front.

He gave me a quick hug and took the bag. "I told you not to bring anything. I see you listened to me, like usual."

The hug was nice. I wasn't so sure about the listening part. I followed him into the kitchen. It looked like Helen's ingredient assembly line when she was cooking, but with even more items. Plates with mounds of several different freshly chopped herbs filled the counter with a flat of eggs next to them.

I remembered how surprised I was the first time I'd seen a carton of eggs as a little girl. "Why are the eggs in boxes, Mommy?" I'd asked.

We collected the eggs from our chickens in wire baskets, and when there was a surplus, we sold them in flats to neighbors. I'd seen them available that way here at the farmers' market, held on Saturday. Scott was clearly learning his way around.

"What can I do to help?" I asked.

"Make yourself comfortable. Would you like some coffee?"

"I'd love some." He had a commercial coffeemaker similar to mine, only much bigger.

"Actually, you can put this pitcher of ice water on the dining room table." He pointed to a door on the other side of the kitchen.

Yesterday, we'd sat in the informal window seat of the kitchen. Today I got to see the main dining area. I entered a high-ceilinged room with wood-paneled walls and large plate-glass windows opening to the back of the property. There were six rectangular tables, each with spacious seating for eight.

Scott had set one of the tables and placed the vase of gladioli from the kitchen in the center of it. Yellow napkins, almost a perfect color match for the tall sprigs of flowers, were neatly folded beside the plates.

The window framing the back pasture let me see that my newfound friend wasn't far away. The little llama peered in my direction. A mural depicting the history of the area covered the opposite wall.

I returned to the kitchen. "Have you named the llamas yet?"

"Named them? Do people name farm animals? Especially ones that spit?"

I laughed. "Yes, they often do. Llamas are kept as pets by many people, and you only have a few of them. Incidentally, they rarely spit at humans. As long as you don't try to eat their food, you should be fine."

"Well, I don't know," he arched an eyebrow at me, "some of those tender bits of grass look pretty tasty." He took a look around. "I think I'm ready. Why don't you name them? There are five females."

"I'll take you up on that. Maybe we'll even enlist the Silver Sentinels."

Car doors slammed, and we went to the front of the house. Martha had parked a white compact car next to the Professor's Mercedes. Scott and I went to the cars to help them unload.

"Mary, is there something I can carry for you?" I asked.

She passed me a foil-covered baking pan. "If you'd take this, that would be great. I'll bring in the second one for Auntie's service so I can put it in the refrigerator."

I peered inside the car. "Where's Princess?"

"We thought it would be best to leave her and Sergeant home with Gertie's son, Stevie, since we weren't familiar with the place. If Martha needs any help, I'm with her."

146 • *Janet Finsilver*

Scott approached Martha. "Hi. I'm Scott Thompson. Kelly told me about you."

"Glad to meet you," Martha said, her voice at a normal level. She must have adjusted her hearing aids. "Thanks for the breakfast invite."

"Glad you could come," he replied.

Scott took the plastic container Gertie had removed from the car, and we all entered the house. The Sentinels chattered happily as they unloaded their wares.

Scott turned on the stove and began melting butter in a large frying pan. "My mise en place is ready." He nodded at the ingredients on the counter. "Time to cook my part of the breakfast."

Gertie and Mary inspected his ingredients on the counter.

"I see you have fresh basil here," Gertie said. "I grow it, and you're welcome to have some anytime you need it."

"Thanks. I appreciate that."

Mary had picked up an unlabeled glass container filled with a mixture of spices. "What's this?"

"A special blend called Scott's Secret," he replied with a smile. "I brought it with me from home."

Mary and Gertie poured a little on a saucer and began inspecting it, calling out various spice names.

"You ladies are good. It doesn't sound like it's much of a secret anymore!"

He cracked eggs into a bowl. The group took their offerings into the dining room while he cooked eggs and bacon. The breakfast party was a success as everyone talked, laughed, and ate. It was a gala event. Mary's fruit crisp had been saved for last.

"Before we partake of dessert, I'd like your help with something," I said.

The group nodded and waited expectantly. While breakfast was being put on the table, I had written on some slips of paper and put them in a bowl.

"You might have noticed we've had some observers while we've been enjoying our food."

Everyone chuckled and looked at the long-nosed, long-necked animals staring over the fence and into the window.

"I'd like to give our new friends names. There are five female llamas, all different in color. I've put those colors on slips of paper.

You get to name the one you pick. Mary and Martha, you can have one for the two of you, and Ivan and Rudy the same."

"What fun!" exclaimed Gertie.

They drew from the container and went outside.

"We got the butterscotch one," Mary said excitedly. "I think we should name her Martha. She looks like she's smiling in a way that reminds me of you."

"Funny, I was thinking Mary would be a good name because of her round cheeks."

"We could call her M and M," Mary said.

Martha snorted. "That's a candy."

"How about Miss M?" Mary countered.

"I like that," Martha said. "What do you think, Miss M?"

The animal batted her long lashes as if in approval. The llama naming was on.

Rudy and Ivan had been quietly conversing with a stately white llama, the largest of the group.

They joined us, and Ivan announced, "We name her Natasha. She is like Russian snow queen in children's tales that *baba*, Grandma, used to tell."

Gertie left her tan charge and showed us the strands of fine hair she held. "I've always wanted to learn to weave. Something new on my horizon. I'm naming her Nell in honor of my aunt, who was a skilled weaver."

The Professor petted the neck of a black llama with a white stripe down her face. "Louisa Mae for Louisa Mae Alcott. They aren't exactly little women, but it would be nice to have a literary touch."

I'd chosen my brown-and-white pal. "I'll name her Annie. All those tight little curls remind me of Orphan Annie."

I went with Mary and Martha to the kitchen to help with dessert. Scott accompanied us.

It was fun seeing his tall frame bent over in serious contemplation next to Mary's short figure, his dark hair next to her white. Scott stood next to her as she slit a vanilla bean lengthwise and scraped its seeds into a milk mixture. After cooking it briefly, she put a spoonful of the crisp into a bowl, added some cream, and handed it to Scott.

"You can be the official taste tester," Mary said.

"Glad to." He took a bite and rolled his eyes in pleasure. "I'd really like this recipe."

"Of course, honey." Mary's dimples popped into view. "I'd be happy to share it. And I'd like the combination of your special-blend spice mixture."

"Deal," he said.

Mary stirred the cream, and Martha put spoonfuls of the crisp on plates. The mingled scent of cooked blueberries, raspberries, and peaches filled the kitchen and made my mouth water. Their colors of blue, red, and gold took the experience to another level. Martha began ladling the cream on the oat-crumb topping.

I put the desserts on a tray and carried them into the dining room, while they took care of putting away what was left. They joined us as I sat down. The conversation consisted of appreciative oohs and ahhs.

Scott sat back. "Thank you all for bringing such wonderful culinary delights. I planned on taking care of you, but I'm the one who got the special treat."

"I beg to differ," the Professor said. "I didn't know scrambled eggs could be so tasty."

The others nodded in agreement.

"I'm glad I'm having a chance to get to know you. I'd love to hear how your group was formed."

Gertie sat up. "We were part of a community group. Some pickpockets were preying on tourists, and we felt we should do something about it."

I'd heard the story before, so I began clearing the table. After a couple of trips to the kitchen, I heard their triumphant conclusion to their first case.

Scott frowned. "Kelly told me what you're working on now. It's a leap to go from catching pickpockets to looking for a murderer."

"We do what is necessary to help our friends and our community," the Professor said.

Rudy folded his napkin and put it on the table. "Auntie and Summer's deaths were deemed an accident because they said Auntie made a mistake."

The Professor sighed. "Just because someone has a few more years on them than most doesn't mean they automatically make mistakes. And yet that's what people often think. That's the conclusion they jump to."

"We know our friends. If we think something isn't right, we check it out. We don't just take it at face value," Mary said. "Auntie wasn't the type to make a mistake. She knew what she was doing."

"We trust our instincts. We want to be sure justice is done for those we care about," Gertie said.

Five serious faces stared at Scott, their hair color white, silver, and steel gray.

"We believe Auntie and Summer were killed. We want to find out who did it, for their sake," the Professor said, "and to prevent the person from harming anyone else."

"Mark called me," Mary said, "and has invited all of us to Summer's memorial service on Monday afternoon at three. Let's talk later about going together."

They all nodded.

Mary continued, "I talked to my friend who manages the botanical gardens. He didn't have anything new to help us. He did tell me they put the topiary donkey in the shed."

I was glad Eeyore had been cared for.

Gertie piped up. "I have news. One of the women in my class called. She told me she saw an older woman meet with Edie for a few minutes, then leave on her own. The two looked a lot alike, and the newcomer was dressed in purple."

"That must've been Sue Ellen," I said. "It means she was out and about by herself during the time of my attack."

Mother and daughter were both without alibis. More small pieces to add to our puzzle.

Chapter 26

Scott offered to take the Silver Sentinels on a tour of what would be the community center. Martha, Mary, and I excused ourselves to attend Auntie's service. We retrieved our food from the refrigerator and went to the parking lot. I got in my Jeep and pulled out, the sisters following me in Martha's white compact.

When I reached the driveway to Despina's cottage, I saw a row of cars parked along one side of the lane, leaving space for one car to pass. I debated about going in or parking out on the road and decided to drive to the house. If there wasn't any place for the car, I could turn around. In my rearview mirror, I saw Martha behind me.

As I reached the clearing, I saw Auntie's sparkling white house with the cornflower blue trim looking like a jewel, with the late-morning sun encasing it. The yellow flowers adorning the porch provided a vivid contrast to the brilliant blue. The backdrop of redwood trees and the lush green meadow framed it like a painting.

A couple of lines of cars occupied the glen, but there was space for us. I parked, and Martha pulled in beside me. I got out and took the cheese plate from the bag behind the seat. Mary joined me, holding her fruit crisp covered in a red plaid dishtowel. Another vehicle arrived as we walked toward the house.

Mary sighed. "I'm going to miss Auntie and Summer. We had some fun and interesting times together. And we were able to help so many people. I hope the sisters will continue her work like they said they would."

"Maybe they'd like your help," I said. "You know many of the people. You could help with the transition."

"Good idea, Kelly. I'll ask them after they've had a chance to settle into the cottage. Maybe I'll do it after Despina's second service, the one that takes place forty days after her passing."

We went by a hummingbird feeder and all ducked as a feathered fighter buzzed over us to shoo a trespasser away from the food. We stopped and watched the iridescent beauty, hovering in place with blurred wings. He eyed us, seemed to feel we weren't a threat, and settled in for a snack.

"It's a treat to observe nature's artwork and be reminded of the beauty that's around us," Martha said. "I believe it's important to appreciate life and the wonderful gifts we receive each day. Auntie and Summer can no longer do that. I think that makes it all the more important that we value every moment we have."

We nodded in agreement, continued on, and went up the steps to the back porch. Since my last visit, a second table had been added next to the counter along the side. Several Despina look-alikes, with their heads covered in black babushkas and wearing matching garments, occupied the chairs, with plates of food in front of them. Greek words filled the air.

We entered and paused at Auntie's shrine. A small photo of her had been placed between the sculpture of Jesus and the miniature Parthenon. A slender bud vase with a single red rose had been put next to it.

We continued into the kitchen. Dishes and pans covered the counters. Trays had been set up on one side to accommodate more food. Fotini was swirling from one side of the room to the other. She saw us, came over, and took Mary's dish.

She pulled back the corner of the cover. "Ahh . . . The fresh fruit. It smells so delicious. We put here."

Fotini somehow managed to tuck it into a space on what appeared to be a completely full counter. Phil's discussion of magic came to mind.

She took the plastic wrap off of mine as I held it. "Please, this can go on the living room table."

I nodded and headed in that direction, Martha and Mary behind me, passing a couple of kids going the other direction in the hallway dressed in what my mom would call their Sunday best. In the parlor, Adrasteia stood at the table where Auntie and Summer had been found. The Book of Secrets lay open on it. Off to my right, a long table held even more food. A rich mixture of aromas spread through the parlor.

"Welcome," Adrasteia said. "I know Despina is pleased all of you were able to come."

"We're glad to be here," Mary replied. "And I was so happy to hear about the Book of Secrets being returned to the family."

"It is back where it belongs." She turned to me. "My sister and I thank you again for finding it for us."

"I'm happy I saw it and knew what it was. Despina probably helped me to be at the right place at the right time."

Adrasteia gestured at the book. "We do not share our formulas or our spells with people not of the immediate family."

Spells? Was there more to Auntie than we knew? Phil had hinted as much.

Adrasteia continued on. "However, there is much more in it. The back shows the owners of the book and their family lineage. Many people here are related or know people in the old country, and we wanted them to have a chance to see it."

I peered at the open back cover. The handwriting varied from generation to generation. Some entries flowed with circles and loops; others were traced with spidery lines. One had bold, dark print that stood out from the others. I moved aside as an elderly man with a cane came up next to me and bent down low to be able to read the book.

Adrasteia said, "There is room on the coffee table for your offering."

I carried the cheese platter into the living room and set it down at the designated place. Martha and Mary came with me. The photos that had been on the table had been grouped on one side. People of all ages filled the room, and all of the couches and chairs were in use.

A woman carrying a tray with shot glasses on it approached the three of us. She held it out. Red liquid glimmered in the glasses, and a pile of biscotti cookies sat on a plate in the center.

A voice at my elbow said, "One of the traditions."

I turned to find Phil.

"The glasses contain wine. You dip the biscotti into the wine and eat it. The biscotti are plain, with a touch of anise."

He proceeded to demonstrate as he took a glass, put the end of the long pastry in the liquid, and ate the piece he had dipped into the glass.

The three of us followed suit. The softened biscotti dissolved in my mouth, the red wine masking any of its flavor.

Phil immersed part of his cookie again. "Depending on the family's tradition, sometimes they serve bourbon."

The shot glasses held only enough wine for three tastes. We put the glasses down and wandered around the room, looking at the photographs on the walls. Despina as a young girl, arm in arm with a young man on her wedding day, one of the same man in military clothes . . . one after another, the photos provided a visual history.

Phil stood next to me and pointed to the last one. "That was Despina's husband. He died in the war. They had no children."

A new row started with the picture I'd seen earlier of her holding the Book of Secrets, with her sisters on either side. A number of other photos of people of various ages reminded me of our family pictures with aunts, uncles, and cousins.

I gazed around the room. There was warmth in the smiles and quiet voices. A sense of positiveness and good feeling pervaded the room. An occasional flash of sadness could be seen, but the gathering was more a celebration, a sharing and remembering of happy times. Because of the sisters' belief that Despina's spirit remained with us for forty days after her death, it was an opportunity to be with her a final time. I didn't understand much of what was said because the majority of it was in Greek.

"Let's go back to the parlor," Mary said. "I'd like to try some of the food people brought."

I went along with the others. If a table could talk—and maybe in this house it could—this one would be groaning. Every inch was occupied by bowls, platters, and dishes. People came and went, helping themselves to a spoonful of this and a helping of that.

Fotini now stood next to the book, and her sister watched over the table, taking away empty containers and adding new offerings. I guessed one of the sisters would be guarding the book at all times, both to protect their secrets and to be sure nothing happened to their family heirloom again.

Adrasteia addressed the group. "Please, everyone, eat. You have all brought such lovely food to share. There's more in the kitchen. You're welcome to go in there as well. Thank you for your generosity."

I saw something that looked like stuffed leaves. "Phil, you're the expert here. Can you tell me what that is"—I pointed to the dish I'd been examining—"and some of the other things?"

"With pleasure." He looked at the food I'd indicated. "Those are dolmas, grape leaves usually stuffed with ground lamb and spices. The dish next to them is moussaka; the main ingredients are eggplant and ground beef topped with cheese."

I thought I could name what was next to the moussaka. "That looks like macaroni and cheese."

Phil looked at me with an expression of feigned indignation. "That is Greek pastichio!" Then he laughed. "Yes, macaroni and cheese. It often has meat in it, but this one doesn't."

We got plates and filled them. I loved events where I could have a sampling of many different foods, most, if not all of them, home-cooked. I'd take a potluck over a fancy meal in a restaurant any day. We found a corner and began tasting.

As I ate, I realized I'd have to leave soon to get to the festival. "Mary, I'll be leaving shortly. Can you take my cheese platter home with you, and I'll pick it up later?"

"Sure, honey. Happy to do it," she replied.

I took a bite of a dolma and glanced around the room.

I froze.

What on earth was Anthony doing here? What connection could he have with Auntie?

Anthony came over to the table and filled a plate with food, a somber look on his face.

I decided I'd see if I could find out why he was here.

I walked up next to him and added another spoonful of moussaka to my plate. "Hi, Anthony. I didn't realize you knew Auntie."

"I did. We'd been . . . working on a project together." He stabbed a dolma with his fork and lifted it onto his plate.

How far could I push this? He hadn't volunteered what they were doing together and had sounded hesitant to share. Well, polite wasn't important where finding a murderer was concerned.

"What was the project?"

Blunt, but if he answered, it might lead somewhere.

"It's something I'd rather not talk about."

Okay. No new path there. A safer topic then.

"Are you working the event today?"

"Yes. I can only stay a little while."

"Same here. There's a nice picture of Auntie over in the shrine you might like to see."

"Yes, I would. Where is it?"

He followed me over to the corner of the room, where Auntie's photo resided in the shrine.

Anthony looked at the portrait, sadness filling his eyes. "Auntie was a good woman, and she had so much wisdom. She was of the old country but willing to work with new ideas. She was a very special person."

I nodded and waited. Maybe he'd say something more.

His hands clenched. "I'm responsible for her death and Summer's."

Chapter 27

I just about choked on the bite of moussaka I'd taken. "How so?"

"A lot of the homeless people I work with have drug problems. I was trying to find a way to shift them off their addictions. Hemlock has been used for medicinal purposes for centuries. It's a sedative and antispasmodic. Auntie and I were trying to find something of a homeopathic nature to help them. Also, some of my hospice patients wanted alternatives to what they were taking."

"So Auntie was using hemlock in her formulas?"

"Yes, at my urging. I went out and picked it for her." He shook his head. "I wish I'd never brought it into her life."

"Did she ever make something you actually gave to someone?"

"No. She was getting close, gathering a lot of information, looking at results online. She was way savvier about the Internet than anyone knew. Not a techie, but she was always looking for ways to learn more and connect with others. We hadn't been working together long, but I took her to a couple of computer classes." He gazed at her picture, then turned his head away. "I wish I'd never asked for her help."

"Anthony, you don't know you're responsible for their deaths."

He turned back to her photo. "I believe I am. She wasn't working with hemlock until we talked. It does look like other herbs, and she was beginning to have problems with her sight." Anthony balled his fists. "I wish, I wish, I wish."

On one hand, I felt for him. On the other, he was still on the list for having a reason to murder Auntie, Summer, and Martha to keep Diane and Ken's marriage from being disclosed. He'd introduced hemlock into Auntie's home. He knew it was there and where it was. She trusted him. He could've laced the tea with it.

I lightly touched his arm. "I'm sorry, Anthony."

"So many times in life you wish you could go back and change something." He shook his head again. "It doesn't work that way."

I looked at my watch. "I need to go. I have to get to the festival."

"I do too," he said and turned away from the shrine. "Maybe I'll see you later at Wine and Flowers."

"Maybe."

I said good-bye to Phil, Mary, and Martha and thanked the sisters for having me. I went to my Jeep and headed for the inn, wondering what Anthony's role was in all of this.

I entered the work area.

Helen was packing up the treats she'd made for the event. "They're almost ready to go."

"Okay. I'm going to change and head to the botanical gardens. I have the first shift at one."

"Did you and the Sentinels have fun at Corrigan's place?"

"Did we ever. Fabulous food and lots of fun naming llamas."

Helen laughed. "Sounds like there's a story there. I look forward to hearing about it sometime."

"Are you going to make it to Wine and Flowers?"

"Yes. I'm taking Tommy and Allie. We plan on going to Phil's dance lesson at two-thirty."

"I'll see you there."

Once in my rooms, I changed into tan slacks and a white blouse. I chose a lightweight navy nylon jacket with the company logo and Redwood Cove Bed-and-Breakfast embroidered on one shoulder. I picked up the manila envelope stuffed with brochures I'd prepared earlier and went to load the car with Helen's brownies. She had packed them in boxes with a generous supply of napkins. They went in my Jeep, along with a small cart.

I drove to the gardens and parked in the vendor lot, unpacked, and began to walk toward the designated area. On my previous visit, I'd been sidetracked by the attack and hadn't made it to the site, but I'd gotten close enough that I felt comfortable I'd be able to find it.

Tank and Anthony were standing with a group of men at the entrance to the visitors' parking lot and appeared to be receiving instructions from a short man in a black cap. Cars started to pull in, and the group dispersed, I assumed to go to their designated areas. It was a relief knowing the two of them had an alibi for the attack on me. I wondered where Daisy was.

I checked in at the counter in the visitors' center and went out through the patio. Ken, Sue Ellen, Edie, and John were seated at the same table they'd been at after the attack on me. A sense of déjà vu was followed by a chill and goose bumps. I avoided eye contact and pulled my cart past them. My next memory flash of yesterday happened as I rounded the corner and viewed the plant version of Winnie the Pooh.

I walked by the stationary animals, wishing they could talk and tell me what they'd seen yesterday. I shuddered as I passed the donkey's sign and the empty space where he'd resided. I was glad Eeyore was stabled in the shed. I certainly hadn't expected to take a wild ride in a donkey.

The slow-moving creek, with its gently swirling water, looked benevolent, not the scene of my near drowning. A duck, with half a dozen yellow, furry balls of fluff following her, floated by.

It was like nature's way of saying, "Really? Something bad happened here? Are you sure you didn't just imagine it?"

I wished it wasn't real, that it had never happened. I felt the vivid memories would be with me for a while.

My area wasn't far away. I left the scene and pushed the unpleasantness to the back of my mind. Rounding a corner and stepping into a sunny meadow filled with flowers and seeing Andy behind a table with mounds of cheese in front of him suddenly made that possible.

He waved, and I walked over to him. An array of cheeses filled the tabletop. The colors ranged from blue-veined to bright orange to creamy white and were formed in wedges, mounds, and slices. Each had a handwritten label and short description.

"Beautiful display, Andy."

"Thanks. I orchestrated it, but the farmers did the work of putting it together. Six places are represented. Their cheeses are all different, so they complement each other but don't compete."

I looked at my watch. "I'd better get set up myself. They'll be letting people in shortly."

"Catch you later," Andy said.

A few tables down, I saw Daniel's tall frame, his shoulder-length ebony hair swinging gently as he moved along the table.

"Hi!" I said and pulled my cart behind the display area.

A crew had put up the tables in the morning, and a volunteer group for the inns had decorated with a blue-green cloth reminiscent of ocean colors. Several abalone shells acting as paperweights flashed their iridescent rainbows. Daniel had weighted down the Ridley House brochures with one and a list detailing the events in the area for the next two months with another. I'd been sent a copy of the activities and looked forward to hearing Daniel's description of them. A rack had information for the other participating inns.

We'd been told by the group who organized the display, Lodgings of Redwood Cove, that our pamphlets would be out all day. The people manning the booth would have theirs on the front of the table while they were there. I unpacked the treats and put out my brochures.

Daniel took a brownie and bit into it. "Another fabulous Helen creation," he said and took another bite.

"She says her baking business is doing really well."

"It's no surprise. Put her cooking skills together with her confectionary artwork, and it's a winner. She'll have a waiting list."

I spied a few people coming down the path and stopping to sample some cheese. "It appears Wine and Flowers is officially open." A few tables down, Scott was talking with several people wearing vests designating them as volunteers. He glanced in my direction and waved. I waved back.

The next hour went quickly, and I learned a lot as Daniel talked about the Crab Fest, the Mushroom Walk, and many other events. Being in a town dedicated to attracting tourists had some real pluses. I served treats and filled paper cups of water from a pitcher. A young man and woman came up and stepped behind the display. They greeted us and said they were the next shift.

Each hour, different food was served by the people manning the table. I packed up what was left of ours and rolled the cart into the grass a few feet behind where we'd been standing.

"Do you think it's okay to leave this here for a while?" I asked Daniel.

"Sure. It's out of the way."

The man putting out pamphlets turned to me. "Definitely no problem for us."

"Thanks."

Daniel put our brochures in the two empty spaces in the rack created by the newcomers removing their information and putting it on display.

"Are you going to see Phil?" Daniel asked.

"I wouldn't miss it. Do you know where his table is?"

"I do. It's in Sunflower Park. Follow me."

The stroll to our next destination was leisurely, as well as tasty. Local restaurants had samples of food from soups to entrées to desserts. Next to each food table was another one with local red and white wines. A musical group performed in each of the settings. A short walk on a path led to the next venue. Depending on the size of the area, six tables or a dozen might be set up.

In one of the larger areas, the Silver Sentinels were spread out at various booths that matched their interests. Gertie was in a deep discussion with a woman at a table heaped with fresh vegetables, while Ivan and Rudy were under a restaurant's banner that said THE BIG FISH.

A sign saying SUNFLOWER PARK let us know we'd arrived at our destination. Phil and a woman manned a table on the far side. Several people with small pours in their wineglasses were in earnest conversation with Phil. Helen, Tommy, and Allie stood at the table next to them with what looked like mini burgers on paper plates.

"What are those?" I asked when I reached them.

"Pork sliders." Tommy finished his in a larger than normal bite.

Helen frowned. "Tommy, you know how to eat properly."

"Sorry, Mom. It's just so good!"

"You should try them," Helen said. "The buns are freshly baked at the Redwood Cove Delectables restaurant."

Breakfast was a while back, and that sounded like a good idea. However, before I could get one, I heard a small band play a couple of notes of a song I recognized, "Never on Sunday."

Phil nodded in their direction, changed the jacket he'd been wearing for a brightly patterned vest, and joined them. The band began playing, and wild, wonderful Greek music filled the air. Phil went into motion, swirling his arms and tapping his feet. People gathered around him, clapping vigorously.

He came twirling next to me and grabbed my hand, and the next thing I knew, we were a line of two. I tapped and moved along with him. A slim woman with her hair pulled back in a ponytail took my other hand. She didn't miss a beat. By the time the song ended, there were six of us, laughing and out of breath.

"Who would like to learn a simple Greek line dance?" Phil asked.

Hands shot in the air, including the Redwood Cove Bed-and-Breakfast group. For the next half hour, Phil walked people through the steps and then danced with them. I helped him, demonstrating for people and partnering with them when we began dancing. Several of the other people who had joined at the beginning did the same.

At the end of the half hour, six good-sized lines of people were weaving their way around the grassy area. The joy on everyone's faces proclaimed the dancing lesson a success.

"Did everyone have a good time?" Phil asked the group.

Enthusiastic cheers and clapping gave him his answer.

"Good. I am glad I had a chance to share with you something of my country." He bowed in several directions. "Now, I must return to work."

Moans, followed by shouts of "Again next year" and "Please do it again" accompanied him back to his table.

He began pouring and talking wine.

I joined the others from the inn. "I'm going to walk around a bit and enjoy this lovely event."

Daniel nodded. "It's fun, and you should introduce yourself. It's a chance to meet a lot of the locals."

"Good idea," I said.

"I'll start back to the car," Helen said. "That'll put me back at the bed-and-breakfast in time to get the appetizers ready."

"I'm going to do the same," Daniel said.

"Mom, can I have some more snacks on our way out?" Tommy asked.

"Three more bites, so choose carefully," she replied.

Allie tugged on Tommy's sleeve. "I remember the chocolate gelato I had last year. The best ever. Save one of your choices for that."

The foursome wandered off, Tommy and Allie with their heads together. Well, as much as that was possible what with Allie being so much taller. They were probably discussing what they were going to eat.

I sampled my way through various offerings, introducing myself each time. People clasped my hand, smiled, and welcomed me. Many invited me to come by and visit their place. A nicer, more pleasant group of people would be hard to find.

Some of the warmth I was feeling dissipated when I rounded a corner and saw Edie painting with a small group of people and an instructor. I almost bumped into her.

She looked up. "Kelly, I found out something you might like to know."

The instructor glanced at us.

"This will be over in about fifteen minutes," Edie whispered. "Can you meet me in the Vista Room?"

Not my favorite place, but if she had another puzzle piece, I was game.

"Sure."

I walked leisurely toward the meeting place, enjoying all the variety at the Wine and Flowers affair. I reached for a cup of Thai shrimp chowder. My purse slipped off my shoulder, jarring my arm. I put the long strap over my head to use as a cross-body strap and pushed the purse around to my side.

The Vista Room was still there. The wooden building hadn't slipped down the cliff yet. A stand describing its history was off to the side of the structure. I went over and read that it had been there for twenty years, so I was probably safe.

I finished the soup, enjoying the combination of lemon grass, coconut milk, and herbs as well as its pungent scent. A sweet, hot flavor lingered on my taste buds. I tossed the paper cup into a recycling bin and took in a deep breath of Redwood Cove perfume—a unique blend of salty ocean air and fragrant flowers.

I entered the Vista Room and went to the wide window. The waves of the blue Pacific Ocean crashed below. I walked around and read the information displayed on the walls, then I checked the time. It'd been about thirty minutes since I'd seen Edie. Where was she? On the bluff off to my right, a slim, blond woman with an easel over her shoulder walked away. Edie. Why wasn't she headed in this direction?

The door closed behind me.

I turned and saw John.

He tugged at the door, and the latch clicked into place.

Chapter 28

My throat constricted at the sound of the click. John was on the list of murder suspects.

I forced myself to sound nonchalant as I said, "Edie said she had something to tell me, but I see her walking away."

"She told me what it was. I said I'd meet with you so she could continue with her painting since it's such a lovely day."

He hadn't moved away from the door.

"What . . . what . . . was it she wanted me to know?"

"It had to do with hemlock. She found some formulas in the fortune teller's book where Auntie had been using it. Rumor has it you and the group we met with believe the two women were murdered."

How had he known that's what we were thinking? I'd been careful to put away the charts. I began to breathe faster.

He laughed, but it wasn't a pleasant sound. "You all think you're so clever, that no one would know what you were up to. The Silver Sentinels have been in the paper, and people know what they do. When they asked neighbors questions about seeing anyone around Auntie's house or what they knew about her right after she died, it was obvious they didn't think it was an accident."

The Sentinels successes had worked against them.

"A number of people from this area work for our dealerships. A few knew Edie wanted to go into business with the fortune teller. My wife was worried you might feel she was involved with their deaths and felt proof Auntie had been using hemlock would indicate accidental poisoning was likely."

It seemed like a good idea to act surprised and grateful at what he thought was new information.

"Thanks. That's good to know. I'll pass it on to the Sentinels. Maybe it *was* an accident." I swallowed hard a couple of times.

He still blocked the entrance to the room.

His cold, almost black eyes bored into me. "Did you follow me to the post office Friday? Did you know something then?"

"I don't know what you're talking about." I edged away from the window and scanned the room for another way out, but saw nothing.

"The money order. You saw it."

"The one for your cousin? All I saw was that it was a money order with a name on it I didn't recognize."

"There is no cousin. I only needed a few more weeks, then it was all going to come together. The investment was due to pay off." He flexed his fingers. "It just took longer than planned, and I had to take out loans on the businesses. The dealerships were doing well, and no one questioned me."

It began to dawn on me. The money order was for him.

"My lunch expeditions patched everything together for a while."

"Lunch expeditions?" My dry throat made it difficult to get the words out.

"You know about me—the Lunch Thief. The Professor snooped around some of the places I robbed. I know because the owners were friends of mine, and they told me about his visits. Stealing from them was easy because I knew their homes. In and out and money in my pocket."

Another desperate search of the room showed no way out but the door.

"The creditors began to call. But I was keeping them at bay . . . until everything froze because of the ridiculous marriage mess. I signed for the letter. As soon as I saw what was in it, I knew there would be problems."

Now I knew who'd received the information, but it wasn't going to help me if I couldn't get out of here. My heart pounded.

"But what threat was there," I asked, "other than there being an additional heir unless you knew there hadn't been a divorce?"

"Ah . . . but I did know that. Ken bragged to me once about his hippie days and dating some rich girl. He said she'd almost tricked him into marrying him, but he said he'd destroyed the marriage certificate and gotten out of that one. What I saw in the envelope said something different."

I remembered the firewood and the fireplace equipment across the room, and I inched in that direction.

"It was easy taking care of the fortune teller and her assistant. I'd been there with Edie, and she'd shown me around." His upper lip curled. "I would have gotten the third one—at least I thought that's who I attacked—if it hadn't been for the stupid dog and your group showing up. Even with the third witness alive, it could've worked, except you persisted with the meeting about the marriage. That's when it all came out."

I felt rooted to the floor. Paralyzed. Like a rabbit being motionless, hoping to escape detection by the hunting predator. But my potential killer knew exactly where I was.

"Ken the Car King, as he so proudly calls himself. I don't want any part of that. I hate the business. I wanted to be in real estate. A respected job, not a position where people expect you to try to cheat them at every turn."

Respected? He'd killed two women.

As if reading my mind, he said, "They went quietly, slowly, peacefully. Dozing off and never waking." He turned away from me and pushed the button on the lock and flipped the dead bolt in place.

When he turned around, his face was that of a different man. It had morphed into a mask of rage—lips tight, face red, and hate pouring from his eyes. His fists balled, and he took a step toward me.

I took a step back.

"You, on the other hand, I'm going to enjoy strangling with my bare hands. Hear you gasp your last breath. You ruined everything."

My peripheral vision showed an iron poker.

"If only you had let it die with those women. Just let it go. But no, you kept digging and digging and digging. You and the others."

He'd started advancing toward me. I went back a step with each one of his in my direction. He lunged, his arms outstretched, hands spread wide. I twirled, grabbed the iron rod, and continued my turn in the same direction, gaining momentum. I swung at his arms. I was never good with a baseball bat, but I was adrenaline-fueled and struck with all my strength. I felt the contact. It went to the bone.

He screamed and jerked his arm away. This gave me a chance to get close enough to have a shot at his head. I stepped forward and swung again. But he was tall, and he saw it coming. John moved back and stumbled into one of the benches. He bent down and pushed it at me, hitting me in the knees.

Pain shot through my legs. I staggered but remained upright. He rammed the bench again, but I had room to sidestep it. He straightened up and started to come at me again.

I grabbed the end of the bench with my left hand and swung it in front of him. He tripped on the foot of the wooden seat. He didn't fall, but he was momentarily off balance. I knew from my training in stick fighting in tae kwon do that the trick was to channel all of your energy through the weapon and to think of going through the object. In this case, the object was John's head. I focused, visualized, and slammed the poker onto the top his head. He fell hard and didn't move. Blood poured down the side of his face.

I didn't wait to see any more. I ran.

I hit the lever of the dead bolt to the side, grabbed the handle on the door, and wrenched it open. As I did so, John moaned, and I glanced over my shoulder. He moved and struggled to one knee.

I still had my purse, thanks to the cross-body strap. I jerked at the zipper as I ran, hoping to get to my phone. No luck. It kept sticking, and I couldn't stop to take time to yank it out.

Sprinting down the trail, I knew the road forked ahead. One route lead to thick crowds of people and safety in numbers, but they were a ways away. The other went to the visitors' center, which was much closer. I glanced over my shoulder. No sign of John. I headed to the main entrance.

As my lungs began to burn and my legs became leaden, I remembered a coach from a long-ago jogging class telling us to pump our arms and forget thinking about our legs; they would follow our arm movements. I pumped.

A turn to the left appeared ahead, and I knew the visitors' center would come into sight. I glanced behind me again. This time I saw John in the distance. There was no sprint left in me, but I wasn't slowing down either. Making the turn, I spied my car in the lot ahead to the right of the building.

People were inside, but who knew what John might do? I kept my car keys in the open side pocket of my purse. I grabbed them out as I ran, ready to hit the unlock button when I got closer. Finally, I was within range. I hit the button, saw the headlights flash, reached the car, and yanked the door open. Throwing myself in, I pulled the door behind me and hit the lock button in one fell swoop.

My hands shook, and the zipper opened in small jerks as I went for my phone. I pulled it out of the inner side pocket and punched in 911.

"What's your emergency?" a voice asked.

"Attacked." My breathing came in ragged gasps. "Being chased."

"Where are you?"

"Redwood Cove Botanical Gardens."

I gave John's name and the type of vehicle he drove.

"I'll dispatch officers now."

Each breath seared my lungs.

I looked out the window. John entered the parking lot. He started toward my car. Without a weapon, I didn't see any way he could get to me. His head jerked up, and he stopped a few feet away. I heard the faint sounds of sirens in the distance. He shook his fist at me, then began to run to his car. He got in, and a few seconds later dust and gravel spun from his tires as he hit the gas hard.

A police car entered the top of the U-shaped parking lot. With a crunching sound, John's vehicle lurched backward out of its spot. He sped past me down the opposite side of the U from the squad car. The officer changed direction and cut across the lawn area at the top of the parking area, cutting John off and blocking his path. John flipped his car around.

In a split second, I made the decision to pull out, blocking his path on my end. If he hit the car, it'd be on the passenger side. Even though he was going fast, it wasn't like he was on a freeway. At best, I'd get a dent, and it might save someone a serious injury caused by a high-speed chase. I inserted the key, started the Jeep, and pulled out in front of him.

He braked, throwing gravel against my window. John had nowhere to go. Parked cars filled the lane on either side of him. The police and I had barricaded him front and back.

Deputy Sheriff Stanton emerged from his squad car, gun drawn. "Get out with your hands up!" he shouted.

John didn't move. Another police car arrived and came around to where I was. I pulled back into my slot and let the officer pull into where I'd been. That officer emerged, gun drawn as well. A third police car joined them.

Still, John didn't come out. I could see his hands on the steering wheel, as could the policemen.

"Keep your gun on him," Stanton said to the other officer.

The man nodded, and Deputy Stanton opened the driver's-side door.

"Out. Now," he said to John. "Hands up."

John appeared in a catatonic state, his movements slow, his eyes blank.

They handcuffed him and put him in the back of the second patrol car.

My lungs felt raw, but I was breathing normally. My trembling hands were another story.

I was alive.

And it was over.

Chapter 29

The police whisked John away. Deputy Sheriff Stanton and one other officer remained.

I got out of my car. "Thank goodness you were able to get here so quickly."

"We have a lot of car break-ins on heavy tourist weekends like this one and at large festivals such as Wine and Flowers. There were more than the usual number of officers in the vicinity."

I told them what happened, and Stanton took notes as usual. Once again we walked down the tranquil botanical garden path. And once again I'd almost lost my life. Only this time it was different. Justice had been done. Despina's spirit could leave in peace after forty days. Perhaps Summer would be with her.

We reached the Vista Room. Even with the officers on either side of me, I hesitated. John's twisted face, like something from a monster movie, filled my mind. Despina might be above, but John was from somewhere down below.

Stanton paused with me. "Ms. Jackson, it'll help if you can go over what happened in the room with us."

"I know."

I took a deep breath, and we went in.

The poker rested on the floor, where I'd dropped it, the blood still wet and red. Its metallic odor permeated the air. A few drops on the floor marked John's path on the way to the door. I reenacted what had happened.

The officers examined the scene, and Stanton said a crew would be arriving to take care of the specifics of photographing and cataloging evidence.

Stanton closed his notepad. "You've had quite the two days."

"You can say that again. Maybe I'd better bone up on my martial arts."

"I have a better idea. Why don't you stay out of the sleuthing business and leave it to the police?"

"But that wasn't happening in this case. The deaths were deemed accidental."

He sighed. "You're right. It wouldn't have been unearthed if you and the Silver Sentinels hadn't persevered." He shook his head. "I'll promise to do less assuming and encourage others on the force to do the same, if you'll promise to keep me informed if you and the others start another investigation of any kind on a case."

"I'll do that."

"Why don't you go ahead and go home?"

Men and women with cameras and black equipment cases arrived. Stanton and the other officer began talking to them.

Home sounded good to me. The festival was winding down. A few stragglers still wandered among the remaining displays. Some of the tables were empty. Vendors packed boxes and carts. I went by and retrieved mine from the booth. A cleanup crew was folding the tablecloth and putting the abalone shells away.

Throbbing told me there'd be bruises on my shins. At least they'd match my ankle. Besides, blue and purple were pretty colors. I smiled wryly to myself. Humor was the best path to take now to leave the drama and darkness behind.

I walked slowly toward the entrance.

"Kelly, wait up," Scott called out.

I did a quick survey of my clothes. Amazing. Nothing torn, no blood, just a little dirt below my knees.

"How did it go?" he asked.

"Fine. I learned about activities in the area, tasted some great food, and met some wonderful people. How about yourself?"

"The people are so excited. I wish Michael could've been here to hear their comments. It's exactly what he'd hoped would happen." He peered at me a little more closely. "Are you okay?"

"Yes, just tired."

I'd tell him what happened eventually, but not now.

"I have the meeting at your place in an hour."

"I know. Helen has it on the calendar for the conference room."

We reached the patio.

"See you in a bit," Scott said.

"Right."

I saw Edie searching the groups of people filing out.

She spied me and came over. "Kelly, have you seen John? I can't find him anywhere. I know he was going to meet you in the Vista Room."

"I did see him, and he gave me your message."

And a lot more. A large container of water sat on one of the wooden tables. I filled two paper cups and handed one to Edie.

"Let's talk."

I sat on the bench. She looked puzzled but followed my lead, putting her painting supplies on the ground. She was about to have her world turned upside down forever. I told her what had happened.

Edie kept shaking her head and saying, "No," interspersed with, "It can't be."

I ended with, "I don't know where the police took him."

Edie didn't move. She just stared at the paper cup. Eventually she raised her head and gazed into the distance.

"He gave me the keys to the shop this morning. An early anniversary present, he said."

I wondered if she needed a ride back to the inn. "Are Ken and Sue Ellen still here?"

"No, they left a while ago." Edie stood. "I need to go to him."

"Are you okay to drive?"

"Yes." She picked up her painting equipment. "It's one of many things I'll be doing on my own now."

Would she be able to take her car, or had the police impounded it? "I don't know if the police have your car or not."

"It's not a problem. I arranged with Anthony earlier to borrow his because of the class. He said he could hitch a ride with his friend Tank. I didn't want John to feel he needed to stay here. He's been covering for a sick manager." Her shoulders sagged. "He won't be doing that anymore."

I remained seated as I watched her leave. I felt someone sit next to me, and a soft, warm hand rested on my forearm.

"You look beat, honey," Mary said.

Little did she know how much that was the truth.

The rest of the Silver Sentinels settled on the bench seats.

"John killed Summer and Auntie," I said and put my arm around

Mary and hugged her. "And he's the one who attacked you." I told the story again.

A short while later I said good-bye to the Silver Sentinels. I rolled my cart to the Jeep, opened the back, and lifted it in. I opened one of the containers and helped myself to a brownie. There was still work ahead of me, and a little chocolate fuel would help. The ride home was short. I put the leftover sweets on the counter and put the cart and the manila envelope with the brochures in the study to deal with later.

I went to my rooms and freshened up. The wall clock said it was close to time for Scott's meeting. I left to be sure everything was ready.

The conference room was designed with an open area at one end so a presenter could put up display tables and work from a podium if they wanted to. We had a stand stored in the closet. Three men stood there—Anthony, Tank, and a young man I recognized from the hot tub. His large dark eyes still darted from side to side. His hands were in constant movement as he twisted the leather strap of the helmet he held in his hands. I recognized it by the color and the flames on the side of it as the one Tank had loaned Daisy.

Just as I thought her name, Daisy bounced in, wearing pink hiking boots tied with shoelaces covered with happy faces. Where on earth had she been able to find those? Our gazes met. She had used less mascara, and I saw she had exceptionally beautiful eyes, green with hazel flecks.

She looked at the men—more specifically, Tank. "Hi! I'll be in the parlor when you're ready to go."

Before Tank could say anything, Ken stormed in, followed by Sue Ellen.

He shook his fist in Tank's face. "You stay away from my daughter. Do you understand?"

"Dad, stop," Daisy shouted.

Tank looked shocked.

"Are you some kind of gym junky trying to look buffed so you can attract girls like her?"

Tank opened his mouth. "I—"

Ken cut him off. "And how is it you carry extra motorcycle gear? Another pickup tactic?"

"I—"

Ken wouldn't let Tank talk. "And your tattoos, what are they of? I see something sharp like a claw coming out from under your sleeve. Do you have some kind of demon inked on your arm?"

"I—"

"Dad, stop saying things like that! You don't even know him." Daisy screamed at him. She grabbed her father's arm and started to cry.

Ken jerked his arm away and pushed on. "Tank. What kind of name is that? Do you barrel your way through and over people? Just who are you anyway?"

"I can answer that," a deep voice said.

While Ken had been ranting, Scott and another man had entered the room. The new person was in an army uniform, ribbons on his chest and a Special Forces tab on his sleeve.

Tank snapped to attention and saluted. "Sir."

The officer returned the salute. "At ease," he said, then looked at Ken. "He's Captain Tank Reynolds. Used to go by Hank, short for Harold, until his men began calling him Tank. That's what he drove during active duty. He and his men were ambushed. He got every one of them out safely, going back time after time. Earned a silver star for bravery. And that's not the only commendation he received."

His voice rumbled with power and strength. "I'm Lieutenant Colonel Madison." His steel-gray eyes bored into Ken. "And who are you?"

The bravado of Ken the Car King was gone. "Ken Nelsen, a car salesman." His hardness, his characteristic pushiness, had disappeared, leaving an uncertain look in his eyes.

Daisy tugged on Tank's arm. "Show him your tattoos."

"Daisy, let's just leave it," Tank said.

"Please," she said.

Those gorgeous eyes did their job. Tank rolled up the sleeve on his right arm. The claw I'd seen was part of a fierce, proud bald eagle resting on a branch, and the slogan above it said "God Bless America." The artist had done a skillful job of making a deep scar on his arm into a branch for the bird to perch on.

"The other one too," Daisy said.

Tank obediently uncovered his left shoulder. An American flag rippled across the muscles of his upper arm. The words "In God We Trust" accompanied this tattoo.

Ken looked like a B-52 had flown over and dropped an emotional bomb.

"Sir, I didn't mean to upset you by seeing Daisy. I didn't know there was a problem," Tank said.

The young man beside him spoke up. "I'm Cole, Tank's brother." He continued to twist the leather strap. "The motorcycle clothes he loaned Daisy were mine."

Ken's face crumpled. "Sorry, Son. It seems I'm not only Ken the car salesman but a jerk and idiot as well." He extended his hand. "I made some assumptions, some wrong ones. I owe you an apology."

The two shook hands and began to talk.

Anthony came over and stood next to me.

"I remember seeing Cole at the hot tub," I said.

He nodded. "He was in the area where some robberies had occurred. You probably know about them. The ones done by someone called the Lunch Thief."

Yes, I did know. Cole had nothing to worry about on that score anymore.

"The police questioned him," Anthony continued. "Cole got scared he'd be blamed and ran away. Tank and I were taking him his medication that day."

I was right about drugs, wrong about the intent.

"He had some bad experiences in the war and has some healing to do."

The dog trainer I had met at Corrigan's place and the Bernese mountain dog he'd been training appeared in the doorway. Tank moved away from Cole and gestured to Ken to follow him. Peter walked over to Tank's brother.

"I'm Peter Wilson, and this is Jake. I hear you've been hoping to get a dog."

Cole nodded, a confused look in his eyes.

He handed the leash to the young man. "He's yours if you want him."

"Mine?" he whispered.

He sank down on his knees next to the big black dog and buried his face in his side. Jake pushed into him. I remembered how soothing it had felt to have the dog close to me. Tears began to stream down Cole's face. Jake licked them away and put his head next to the dark-haired man.

Peter smiled. "There's some paperwork to do, but there's no reason he can't be with you from now on. He's PTSD-trained. Tank helped me know what we needed to teach him to be your companion."

Cole looked at him and nodded. The tears kept coming.

I guessed he couldn't speak right now. I was on the verge of crying along with him, and I would've had trouble talking right then.

"Your cabin at Michael Corrigan's place is all ready," Peter said. "I'll work with the two of you for a few days so you can learn his commands and how he responds in different situations. We can fine-tune his skills to fit your needs."

Cole nodded again and stood up, clenching the leash. The twisting hands and darting eyes were gone.

Jake didn't take his eyes off him.

They were a match, the rescuer and the rescued. It didn't matter who rescued whom.

Chapter 30

Scott spoke up. "Cole and Tank are going to help develop the area to be occupied by veterans. They'll both live on-site."

Tank put his arm around Cole's shoulders. "Jake has a K-nine phone he's been trained to use if you have one of your seizures, or you can command him to call if you need something. It has my number, and I'll be in the cabin next to you."

"Anthony will be nearby as well," Scott said. "A number of the homeless men in the area are veterans. He'll be working with them and seeing if we can bring some of them into the center."

Anthony nodded. "I'll be in the cabin area for a while. Then the plan is for me to move to the main house."

"Anthony is skilled at communication," Scott said. "He'll be doing general community outreach as well."

"I bet the Silver Sentinels can help him with the names of people who would be good for him to contact," I said.

"I know they can. We talked about it when we toured the place." Scott turned to the lieutenant colonel. "I know your time is limited. I appreciate your coming today to meet and talk about our plans."

I took that as my cue to leave. I started toward Ken and Sue Ellen to nudge them out of the room. As it turned out, I didn't need to do that. Deputy Sheriff Stanton arrived. I knew what he had to tell them.

"I'm looking for Mr. and Mrs. Nelsen," he said.

"Here," Ken said, looking puzzled.

"I need to talk to you."

Ken frowned. "Sure. We have a sitting area in our rooms we can use."

They departed. They too were about to find their lives in upheaval. I wondered how much damage John had done to their business.

The men began to seat themselves at the table. Cole and Jake appeared to be glued to each other. The looks that passed between them showed mutual adoration. Tank's brother's demeanor had changed just in the short time he was with his new companion. I excused myself.

I went to the work area, sat at the counter, and suddenly felt like I couldn't move. I was so tired. Helen was busy with the cheese and wine time for the guests, taking out plates and bringing in dirty dishes.

"You look beat," she said as she put a platter in the sink.

It was the second time someone had said that. It must really show.

"It's been a long day but a gratifying one."

I told her about Cole and his PTSD dog. I didn't get into any details regarding John.

"It's wonderful to hear the young man has a new chapter in his life ahead of him."

"I agree. Michael is doing so much to help people. Maybe I'll call him and let him know what a profound effect he's already having."

I went to my rooms, passing the conference area on the way. The door was closed, and I heard talking. The group was making plans for more people to have a fresh start in life. I poured a glass of Pellegrino and dialed my boss.

"Kelly, good to hear your voice. How are you settling in?"

"I love it, Michael. I wanted to tell you about something I saw this afternoon that you are responsible for. You changed someone's life."

I told him in detail about what had taken place. He was a dog lover, and the fact that Jake was a rescue made everything that much more special.

"Thanks for calling, Kelly. It really means a lot to hear it from someone who was there when they met. I hope we can do it for many more people and dogs."

"Scott has put together a great group in Tank, his brother, Cole, and Anthony."

"I was surprised when Scott took the assignment. With his cosmopolitan background, it didn't seem like it would be a fit."

This stumped me for a moment. What should I say? I wasn't prepared to talk about anything personal.

"He said he wanted to try something new," I replied.

True. I didn't have to say anything about him mentioning me.

"I see," he said.

And Corrigan probably did see. I thought I heard a chuckle.

"How are the Silver Sentinels doing?"

I brought him up to speed on what had happened.

"Just how many murders can a small town like that have?" he asked.

"Hopefully, no more."

We ended the call. My cell phone rang before I had time to leave the room. I didn't recognize the number.

"Hello," I answered.

"Kelly, it's Diane Purcelli. I wanted to thank you. I met with Mark."

"How did it go?"

"Wonderful. He's a very sweet man. We look forward to getting to know each other. He has no anger toward me. Summer was his mother as far as he's concerned, so he doesn't feel like he missed out on anything in life. Thank you so much for helping to make this happen."

"You're welcome. Have plans been made to help him with his medical condition?"

"Absolutely. He's coming to San Francisco to a specialty clinic. It's named after his grandfather, making it even more fitting he should be treated there. Thank you again."

"You're welcome."

Summer would have been very pleased.

I went to the parlor to check on the guests. Daisy was off in a far corner, thumbs flying over her phone. Sue Ellen and Ken sat on the couch in front of the fireplace. I went over to pick up their empty dishes just as Ken reached out and took his wife's hand.

"Sue Ellen, who have I become? What have I become?" He squeezed her hand. "I was so wrong about the young man Daisy is seeing. I've been wrong about other things as well."

He gazed at her with a look of sincerity and affection I hadn't seen before. I grabbed their plates and turned to leave.

"No, wait," Ken said. "I treated Sue Ellen poorly in front of you. I'd like you to hear what I have to say."

Uh, oh. There was still more involvement with this family ahead of me.

Ken turned to his wife. "I've been a cold, hard, heartless, selfish human being to you and others. I'm sorry. I'll agree to the divorce you wanted. Your terms. I understand why you want to leave."

I shifted uncomfortably from one foot to the other.

Sue Ellen shook her head. "I don't want a divorce. I just want us to be together like we used to be."

He rested his hand on her knee. "I haven't always been like this, have I?"

Oh boy, did I want out of here. I opened my mouth to excuse myself, but Sue Ellen beat me.

"No, Ken. You fought hard to develop your business." She patted his hand. "You took care of your family. Maybe you developed some calluses along the way, got some bruises from being knocked around a bit."

"I need to learn to be more like my son, Anthony."

Sue Ellen put her arm around him. "You are a caring, loving father."

"I don't know what's ahead of us financially, how much damage John did to our business," Ken said.

"We worked long hours before, we can do it again." Sue Ellen leaned into him. "I have a lot of good memories about those times."

Time to leave. "I hope you liked your rooms."

Before they could reply, I made my exit and deposited their plates in the sink. I rinsed them and put them in the dishwasher, thinking about the conversation I'd just heard. Their son-in-law was a murderer, and who knew what he had done to their business. They had a long road ahead.

I heard voices in the hallway indicating the meeting with Scott was over. I followed the sounds into the parlor. Sue Ellen and Ken were gone.

Daisy was front and center. "I'm ready for our hike," she said to Tank.

He laughed and looked at the rest of us. "It's a walk on the headlands."

"Sounds like a hike to me," she said.

"It probably does." He looked at her with affection, seeing something in her I'd missed.

Daisy smiled at him. "Do you think Cole and Jake would like to join us?"

What? Daisy thinking of others?

"Why don't you ask him?"

Daisy went over to Tank's brother, who had settled on the floor in the corner of the room with Jake next to him.

"Would you like to join us for a walk?'

Cole looked at his new companion and back at Daisy. "Yes. That would be nice."

He stood, and Jake wagged his tail enthusiastically. The four of them left.

Scott thanked the lieutenant colonel and said he'd be in touch. The officer nodded at me and departed.

Scott addressed Anthony. "The meeting went well. I'll call you tomorrow, and we'll begin to put together a plan."

"Okay. I'm going to the hot tub and see if any of the homeless are there."

"Wait," I said. "We have leftover brownies."

I hurried to the kitchen and returned with the box.

"They'll love these," Anthony said. "I'll definitely score some points."

Anthony left with the treats, and Scott and I went to the kitchen.

"Why don't I run to the market and put together one of our deli dinners?" he suggested.

I smiled at him. "I'd like that. I'll set the table."

We didn't discuss food choices. Scott had done fine the times we'd done this before. I watched his tall figure through the back window as he walked down the driveway.

Movement outside caught my eye. Tommy and Fred were in the front yard of their cottage having what looked like a jumping contest to see who could go straight up in the air the highest.

Daniel's Volkswagen bus arrived, and he and Allie got out. I remembered they'd mentioned something about extended family Sundays and invited me to join them. Dinner together. Movies and games. Tonight dinner was with Scott, but I looked forward to Sundays with the others.

Ken and Sue Ellen were rebuilding their lives.

I was ready to create my new one.

ABOUT THE AUTHOR

Janet Finsilver and her husband live in the San Francisco Bay Area. She loves animals and has two dogs—Kylie and Ellie. Janet enjoys horseback riding, snow skiing, and cooking. She is currently working on her next Redwood Cove mystery. Readers can visit her website at www.JanetFinsilver.com.

First in a new series!

Murder at Redwood Cove

A stay at this B & B may be permanent...

Janet Finsilver

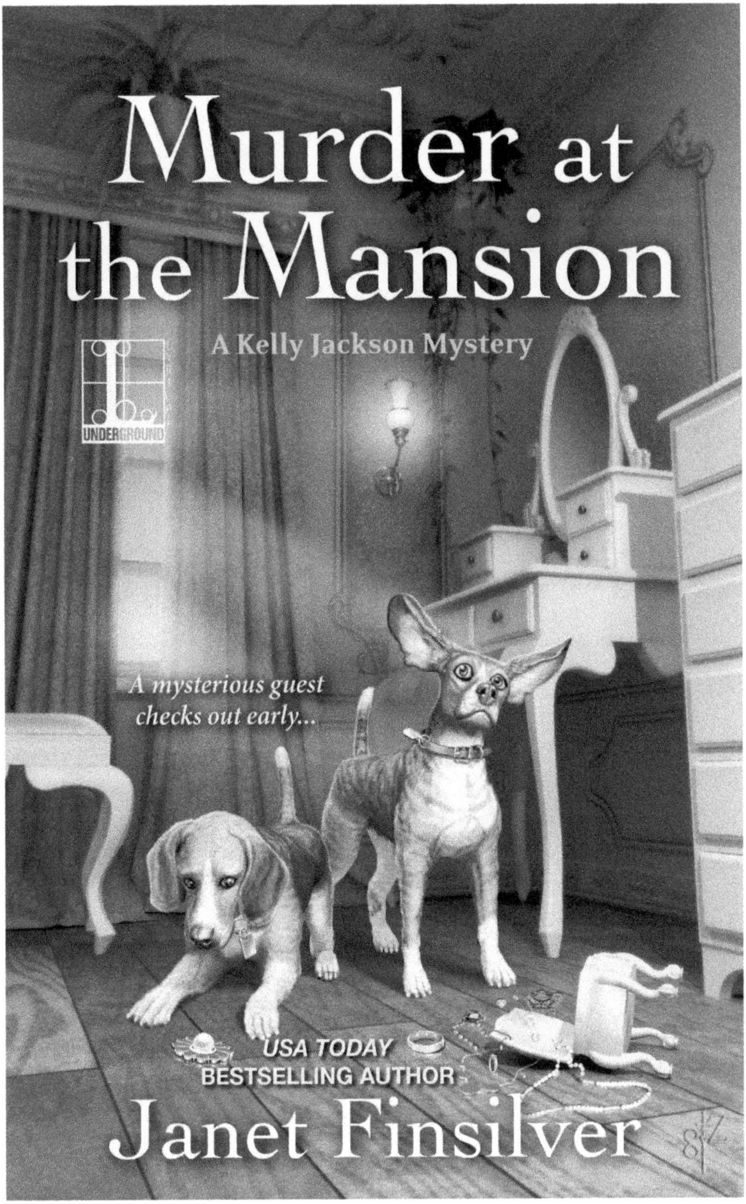
Murder at the Mansion
A Kelly Jackson Mystery
UNDERGROUND
A mysterious guest checks out early...
USA TODAY
BESTSELLING AUTHOR
Janet Finsilver

CPSIA information can be obtained
at www.ICGtesting.com
Printed in the USA
BVHW07s1544240918
528340BV00002B/276/P